P9-CCL-082

OVERTIME

Faith looked up at Gerard, smiling. "I've decided we're going to have a son first. I just dreamed we had one. Maybe that was a premonition," she added. "We'll name him after you."

Tumbling on the sand, they shared kisses.

Pinning Faith beneath him, Gerard stared at her with a wry grin. "Suppose we have a girl first. Do you plan on sending her back?" he teased.

"You keep on doing your part, and I'll guarantee the rest," she declared. "If we have a girl, we have to return to Project Baby until we produce a boy to carry your name."

Gerard laughed heartily. "You are too much." Nuzzling her neck with kisses, he said, "I'm ready to put some overtime in on whatever it is you want."

Stronger
Than
Yesterday

NICOLE KNIGHT

LEISURE BOOKS NEW YORK CITY

*To my loving and supportive husband, Edward,
and
my children, Ted, Kevin, and Kim.*

A LEISURE BOOK®

May 2006

Published by

Dorchester Publishing Co., Inc.
200 Madison Avenue
New York, NY 10016

If you purchased this book without a cover you should be aware that this book is stolen property. It was reported as "unsold and destroyed" to the publisher and neither the author nor the publisher has received any payment for this "stripped book."

Copyright © 2006 by Nicole Knight

All rights reserved. No part of this book may be reproduced or transmitted in any form or by any electronic or mechanical means, including photocopying, recording or by any information storage and retrieval system, without the written permission of the publisher, except where permitted by law.

ISBN 0-8439-5660-7

The name "Leisure Books" and the stylized "L" with design are trademarks of Dorchester Publishing Co., Inc.

Printed in the United States of America.

Visit us on the web at www.dorchesterpub.com.

STRONGER THAN YESTERDAY

CHAPTER ONE

Faith Parker-Wynn sat on a blanket spread on the ground beneath a shade tree, watching her husband, Gerard, and their child having the time of their lives tossing a Frisbee back and forth. Their five-year-old son rolled his eyes in frustration because he hadn't been able to catch the toy his father flung his way. With Gerard's patience and instructions, Gerard, Jr. ran and leaped to finally catch it successfully. Each time the boy accomplished this feat, his face radiated with pride. His father shouted encouragement whenever his son made a catch. Smiling at her two men, Faith rubbed her swelling tummy. The baby within wiggled as though she shared in the delight her mother experienced on this summer day.

After a while, Gerard joined Faith on the blanket. Sitting beside her, he rested his hand on her stomach and caressed it tenderly. "Are you comfortable? If you aren't, we can leave."

1

"I'm fine. It's a beautiful day, and I want to enjoy it. Besides, Junior is with a friend, and he doesn't look as though he's ready to go either." She eyed her son as he made his way toward the playground area with a neighborhood boy who had shown up. "Junior, be careful," Faith called to her son.

"He'll be fine," Gerard assured her.

"That kid plays a bit too rough sometimes. Junior always ends up with a scrape or a bruise when he's with that child."

Gerard shrugged. "Boys will be boys. He's growing up, and you can't smother him, Faith."

"He's still my baby, and I'm going to always worry about him."

Gerard chuckled softly. "Look at your baby now."

"Oh my goodness," Faith declared, watching Gerard, Jr. take on his playmate as though he were a wrestler from the world wrestling show he and his father viewed. Her son was attempting to lift the boy. "Go get that child."

Gerard hopped up and ran toward their son.

Observing her husband joining the two boys in play, Faith began to laugh. Gerard had let the two boys get him on the ground. They'd climbed on top of him and made noises as they feigned punches.

Life couldn't be sweeter. Faith sighed.

Gerard awakened Faith from her dream by dropping down beside her on the sands of the Jamaican beach and placing a kiss on her lips.

Her eyes fluttered open, revealing a delightful twinkle in their light brown color. Her mouth eased into a marvelous smile. "I was dreaming about us and our kids."

Pulling Faith to him, Gerard asked, "You've made me a father already?" He wrapped his arms around her shoulders and rested his face next to hers.

"Only in a dream, for the moment." She laughed softly.

Gerard inhaled the fresh air. "I've gotten spoiled here in this paradise with you. When I return to the bank, I won't be able to concentrate the way I should. Images of you and me and the love we've made here are going to be coursing through my mind." He kissed the side of her mouth, tickling her lips with his tongue. "I don't want to go back to the real world," he said, sighing.

Faith grinned. "Neither do I, but we have to get on with our lives and prepare for our future." She gazed out at the ocean, feeling bubbly and full of life. "I can't remember when I've ever felt more relaxed or more desirable. This time together has made it even clearer to me why I love you so much."

Turning Faith toward him, Gerard gazed at her lovely face. When they'd arrived on the island eight days ago, he'd adored the fact she hadn't fussed with her hair or makeup. She would get up in the morning, shower and wash her hair, then let it dry into natural crinkly curls that made her look like a college coed. He appreciated the way her honey complexion maintained a flushed rosy color from their sweet intimacy. He also noticed how much more comfortable she was with her body. When she walked, she had a sexy swagger to her hips that showed she was proud of being a woman.

Placing a kiss on her forehead, Gerard said, "Baby, I love you too. I'm glad I'm your man." He held her more tightly.

In the circle of his arms, Faith relished the strength of her husband's love. Brushing her cheek against his face, she murmured, "I feel the same way too. There's only one thing that could make me happier."

"Tell me what that is, so I can make it yours. I intend to spend the rest of my life keeping you on cloud nine," he said in a sensual tone.

"You already know I stopped using birth control a couple of months before our wedding, and I just had a dream about us having kids." She intertwined her fingers with his.

"If you haven't become a mommy since we've been here, then it will be a miracle. We've been working a lot of overtime on this little project." He laughed. "I'm sure we'll have a lifetime souvenir from our honeymoon.'

Her eyes sparkled with anticipation. "Let's hope things work out the way we want."

Searching Faith's face, Gerard said, "I want to

begin a family as badly as you, but I have to admit I'm concerned about a few things."

Faith turned slightly toward him. "In what way?"

"How are you going to manage a pregnancy along with the stress of running Fabulous and working with Morning Has Broken?" he asked, referring to Faith's business and her civic organization. "Along with my long hours at the bank, a baby will really have us on our toes. Are you ready for our love to be challenged with all the responsibilities of parenthood?"

"I'm all set," she said with certainty. "A baby will enhance what we already have. I truly believe there is nothing you and I can't do as long as we love each other."

"I'm glad you're ready, angel."

Turning to Gerard, Faith looped her arms around his neck and rested her forehead against his. "Gerard, I have to get in the baby business now. I'm thirty years old."

"My old lady," he teased.

"Don't call me that." She looked up at him, smiling. She let out a contemplative sigh. "I've decided we're going to have a son first. I just dreamed we had one. Maybe that was a premonition," she added. "We'll name him after you."

Tumbling on the sand, they shared kisses.

Pinning Faith beneath him, Gerard stared at her with a wry grin. "Suppose we have a girl first. Do you plan on sending her back?" he teased.

"You keep on doing your part, and I'll guarantee the rest," she declared. "If we have a girl, we have to return to Project Baby until we produce a boy to carry your name."

Gerard laughed heartily. "You are too much." Nuzzling her neck with kisses, he said, "I'm ready to put some overtime in on whatever it is you want."

Faith engaged him in a heated openmouthed kiss. She gazed at him, appreciating the way the light of the full moon defined his well-chiseled face. His profile spoke of his power and strength, which she found appealing. She loved the lusty expression reflected in his pecan complexion. His unbuttoned tropical shirt allowed her to slip her arms around his bare chest.

He eased his hands beneath her sundress, caressing her thighs, then her bottom. Gerard's eyes widened with delight when he discovered she was pantyless. "You're turning into a sex kitten." Laughing lustily, he placed wet kisses along her neck and across her chest.

Lowering her hands inside the back of his shorts, she discovered he wore no underwear either. "Oh my." She giggled. "This is going to be one unforgettable night. What a perfect ending to our honeymoon." As she relished the heat of his breath and the way his tongue slid over and around hers, a moan of satisfaction escaped her lips. "You are everything to me," she cooed between kisses. Heat and moistness settled in her

6

feminine cove. Gerard tugged down the top of her dress, exposing her luscious, pert breasts, and Faith lifted her shoulders, aiming her erect nipples toward his mouth.

Gerard's eyes gleamed at the sight of her exquisite breasts. Catching a glimpse of the dizzying expression of passion on his wife's face, Gerard studied her as though she were a celestial being. "You are so beautiful at this moment," he declared in awe.

She inhaled deeply, as though her joy made it difficult to breathe. Enchanted, she smiled at him. Removing her dress, she parted her legs, inviting him to unite them for a lovers' journey.

Gerard grew light-headed from her teasing, which never ceased to mesmerize him. He stroked her feminine essence as though it were priceless silk. She wriggled against his touch and whimpered from her excitement, making him weak with wanting. Fitting himself between her thighs, he eased his ready arousal inside her.

Gerard gazed at his wife's face. Her beauty and sensuality pushed his restraint to its limits. It took everything in him to keep from reaching his climax right then. As his urgency brewed, his kisses and touches grew more fervent.

Gerard locked his arms around his wife's waist to intensify their loving. He lifted her legs around his hips and pushed himself deep inside her hot softness. He caused her to cry out, and she quivered from their rapture. He held her tightly, shuddering and groaning, drowning in the whirlpool of glorious ecstasy they'd created.

In the afterglow of love, Faith and Gerard lay together on the sand, embracing and laughing softly at the wonders and the magic they'd shared.

They hadn't been resting long when voices and laughter could be heard from an approaching group.

Faith pushed her husband away. "Oh goodness, people are coming this way. We have to get dressed." She reached for her dress. Sitting upright, she eased it over her feet and up her body. "Gerard, grab your shorts," she ordered frantically.

Gerard remained on the sand, unclothed and grinning. "Chill, baby. Nudity isn't an issue for me. I'm proud of my body, and you should feel the same about yours. Besides, we don't know anyone here. Who cares if they see us?"

Faith stood, arms akimbo, over him. "I bet if we were back in Bellamy, you'd be worried. Since we've been here, I've met a few women in the spa at the hotel. When I saw them, they told me they were going partying at this club on the beach. Don't embarrass me this way," she pleaded. "Gerard Leonard Wynn, get into those clothes now! You will not ruin our honeymoon by shaming me with your indecent exposure." She glanced over her shoulder and could see the group she assumed to be club-hoppers getting nearer. Panicking, Faith picked up his shirt and shorts and laid them over his genitals. "You're incorrigible. I can't believe you," she said. She dropped down next to him and leaned across his lap as the small group passed them. Two of the women in the group called out to Faith in a manner that revealed they were inebriated, not only from liquor but also from their festive mood. Faith spoke politely, and the revelers proceeded down the beach.

Once the people had passed, Gerard cradled her in his arms and let out a hearty laugh. He kissed her, and hugged her tightly.

Though Faith was annoyed, she couldn't resist joining in his laughter. She returned his embrace. "Will you get dressed now that you've almost humiliated me? We need to shower and get some rest. We have to get up in a couple of hours to pack for our flight back to the real world."

"Yes, ma'am," he said, releasing her. Once he was clothed, Gerard swept her up in his arms and carried her back to their hotel.

His gallant action made Faith feel as though she were a princess in a fairy tale, destined to live happily ever after. Hugging him around his neck, she truly believed they would have a great life as husband and wife. Why shouldn't they? she mused, resting her head on his shoulder. Hadn't she been blessed enough to find her prince?

CHAPTER TWO

Gerard had been home in Virginia for three days when he decided to stop by his old house. He needed to pick up his mail and some boxes to take to his new residence.

Parking in front of the town house where he had lived for years with his best friend, Alex Washington, Gerard was glad to see Alex's car in the driveway. Gerard used his key to enter. Once he was inside, he called out to Alex, who let him know he was in the den.

"Hey, Mr. Commitment. What's up?" Alex asked, grinning. He sat forward in his recliner.

"Man, don't hate. You know you're jealous because you haven't found a woman who is as fine as mine," Gerard said. He dropped down on the nearest chair and eyed the television, which played the latest ESPN programming. "I came by to get the rest of my stuff. What are you going to do with an extra bedroom?"

"I'd better keep it available for you as a dog-house." Alex laughed. "You're bound to do something to tick the little lady off."

Gerard chortled. "Man, you're such a hater. Go on and turn it into an office or game room. I won't be needing it," he said with confidence.

"I've got some cold beer. You want some?" Alex asked.

"Not now." Gerard settled back in his chair. "Where's the mail you said came for me?"

"It's in the hallway where we always kept our mail, man," Alex said, returning his attention to the television as the sportscaster reported on the latest triumph of his favorite team.

Gerard went in the hallway and returned with his mail. He flipped through it quickly.

"Marriage agrees with you. You look good," Alex said.

"So far so good," Gerard said. "You ought to give it a try. You're getting too old to be a player."

Alex laughed. "I'm not ready for a ball and chain yet. I like my freedom."

"You're too much," Gerard said, "I never thought I'd get married again after my first one failed. I had hooked up with the wrong woman for all the wrong reasons."

"Iris Burton. The first woman you got to first base with."

"Yeah, I was too young to get married."

"Man, she had you twisted." Alex shook his head. "You got sex and love all mixed up."

"Yeah, I was confused, I admit it. I didn't have my choice of ladies the way you did in college. I was such a geek," Gerard said, shaking his head.

"That woman had you stupid," Alex continued. "I tried to school you, but you'd get mad with me. Then after Iris started showing you her true colors, you understood what I was telling you."

"The less said about it, the better it is. I got me a good woman who I know loves me, and I sure as hell love her."

"Listen to you." Alex's eyes flashed with amusement. "You sound whipped, man. Does this mean you won't be hanging out with me and the fellas anymore?"

"Well, not anytime soon. I owe my wife some quality time to get this marriage off on the right foot."

Alex nodded and smiled wryly. "Mr. Commitment."

"That's who I am, and I'm proud of it," Gerard said. "By the way, Faith told me she expects to see you at the Bellamy Square Mall when her women's group for Morning Has Broken have their fund-raiser. They'll be selling all kinds of merchandise and accepting donations for a building site. She wants you to spread the word of the event to your coworkers and friends to come too."

"Oh man, what's this? Not only is she running you, but she's trying to run me too," he teased.

"You'd better make it. Faith doesn't play. You won't be welcomed at our house."

"I'll be there. I can't afford to make you look bad. She knows some fine sisters in some of those organizations she's all mixed up in. Maybe she can put a good word with one of them for me."

"The only way Faith is going to put in a good word for you is if she thinks you have good intentions toward her friends. She's not going to let you play any of her girls," Gerard said.

"Boss lady is something else. She knows I have eyes for that fine soror of hers Eva Carey. I only wish I was a kid, so I could be a patient of that pediatrician."

Gerard was amused by the smitten look on his friend's face. He wasn't used to seeing him that way. Alex, with his charm and good looks, usually had his pick of women, but this Eva was different. She hadn't been fazed by Gerard's friend. She was far too busy with her practice and a life nearly as busy as Faith's with civic and community activities.

"I'm glad I'm not in your shoes. I have my gem. I should be getting home to her now." Gerard got up to leave. "My wife is cooking dinner, and I don't want to be late. Help me carry my things to the car."

Alex got up and followed Gerard to his old bedroom.

Once the last box had been stuffed into the trunk, Alex shoved his hands in the pockets of his jeans. "Man, I know I've been kidding you about this marriage business, but I'm happy for you.

You got yourself a good lady. You deserve all the happiness I see on your face. I envy you."

"You envy me?" Gerard asked, skeptically eyeing his usually carefree friend.

"I'm for real. I know all the ladies love me, but that's getting kind of old." He rubbed the back of his neck. "If I can find that special lady, I might do the marriage thing, too."

"I never thought I'd see the day you'd get soft on me." Gerard slapped him on the back.

Alex jumped back and lifted his fist, feigning annoyance. "If you tell anybody what I just said, I'm going to have to hurt you."

"Easy, dude. Your secret is safe with me," Gerard said, grinning. "I'm out of here. I'll be in touch." He walked to the side of his car.

"Yeah. Make sure you tell Faith I'll be at the fund-raiser. I don't want to lose my visiting privileges. If Dr. Eva Carey is there, I might get very generous with my checkbook."

"You're such a clown. But I'll pass the word to my wife," Gerard said from inside his car, and honked the horn before pulling off.

Although Gerard had been coming home to his large new brick house in the suburbs for the past few days, his heart still filled with pride and anticipation. He had come a long way from the lonely and confused boy whose mother had deserted him and left him to be raised by his grandmother. Gerard remembered the neighborhood

15

composed of a hundred worn cinder block homes with small patches of dirt for yards. The area was riddled with crime and hoodlums.

His grandmother had kept a watchful eye on him and encouraged him to focus on his school-work. His grandmother hadn't wanted him to become a victim of drugs or of the numerous shootings that took place all too often in the vicinity. The only place Gerard was allowed to play was at the Boys Club, which was well supervised by people she knew would set a good example for her abandoned grandchild. Gerard felt as though the place was his second home. As he grew into a teen, he became a mentor to younger boys, an achievement of which his grandmother was truly proud.

The old neighborhood where he and his grandmother had lived had been demolished to make way for businesses. His grandmother Estelle now lived in a high-rise retirement home that Gerard had found for her. There, she lived in safety and was able to enjoy herself with all kinds of activities and outings with other seniors.

Coming from where he had, Gerard was thrilled by the fact that he had a chance to build a life, to have kids and to share a future of happiness and love with a woman like Faith. It was a childhood dream come true. Growing up and being reared by his loving grandmother, he had never known the love and attention of his mother, which couldn't be replaced even by the care he had been given. And, sadly, he'd never had a chance to know who his father was.

"Baby, I'm home," Gerard called out, entering the house.

Faith hurried from the kitchen, wearing a pink lounging pants outfit. She greeted him with a kiss and a snug embrace.

"You smell so good," he said. He pressed his nose against her neck, intoxicated by her fresh, clean scent.

"I rushed home from the store and took a shower before I began cooking dinner," she explained, taking him by the hand and leading him into the kitchen. "I was expecting you a little earlier. Where have you been?"

"I stopped by my old place to pick up the last of my things, and Alex and I got to talking." Gerard's nose tingled from the delicious aroma of the food. He visibly admired the table set for two and the centerpiece of roses in a vase. He took a seat at the table.

"Did you mention the fund-raiser?" Faith asked.

"I sure did. You can count on him." Gerard eyed the food. "Don't tell me you fried chicken," he said, admiring the golden pieces.

"I sure did. Not only did I do chicken, but I also made macaroni and cheese and corn bread from scratch. We have collard greens too. I can't take credit for those because they're canned, but I seasoned them to make them taste as close to home-made as possible." She grinned with pride, pouring him a tall glass of tea.

"A soul feast for a king. You're spoiling me," he said, taking a piece of chicken and biting into it. "Mmm . . . this is good, baby."

Faith smiled appreciatively and gave him hearty servings of the other dishes.

Gerard was pleased by Faith's effort in preparing a full-course meal. He knew she could cook, but when they were dating, she'd hardly had time to spend in the kitchen. There had been some dinners she'd taken time to prepare, including his birthdays and anniversary celebrations, before they got engaged. Other than that, they usually went out or picked up take-out food.

Over dinner they chatted about the events of their days. Afterward, Gerard helped her to clear the dishes and place them in the dishwasher. They retired to the living room, where Faith brought out the packets of pictures of their honeymoon she had picked up that day from Wal-Mart. Faith sat on Gerard's lap while they relived their blissful time in Jamaica.

The pictures had come out clear and showed them posing for each other, from silly posturing to sensual, against the gorgeous backdrop of blue skies and the flowers, the people who call paradise their home. Then there were some they had snapped of each other that reflected the handsomeness of Gerard and Faith's striking beauty.

There were also loving shots of them in front of various historic sites and on the beach, taken by tourists whom they had drafted to use their camera. While Faith and Gerard studied the pictures, they kissed and reminisced about the sights from their romantic escapade.

"I've bought an album especially for these," she said. "Along with our wedding pictures, these will begin the history of our marriage."

Gerard kissed her tenderly. "I truly love you."

"I know." She gazed into his eyes.

"You're going to take advantage of me. You're going to make me spoil you, aren't you?" He began to tickle her until she begged for mercy in between her breathless laughter.

"Since I spent part of my day sweating in a hot kitchen over dinner, the least you can do is to give me dessert," she said in a sultry tone.

"Oh, I've got dessert for you," he said. "You're going to love it." He carried her to their bedroom.

Once they reached the room, Gerard dumped her on the bed in a playful manner. "Strip, woman," he ordered, standing with his hands on his hips.

Faith fell into her role as submissive vixen. "Yes, sir, right away." She knelt on the bed and began stripping away the jogging suit she wore, revealing her lack of underwear.

Gerard's eyes gleamed as he examined her luscious golden flesh, and the sight of her perfect breasts made his bulging arousal ache. To further tease him, his wife lay upon the bed on her stomach, with a look of mischief on her face.

"It's your turn. Showtime, playa. Give me a show that will make my goodies even sweeter for you." She gave him a smoldering look and licked her lips to further entice him.

Joining in the fun between them, Gerard turned his back and set to removing his business attire of shirt and tie and slacks piece by piece, as if he were in a strip club. When he had gotten down to his boxers, he turned to face her and did a bump and grind as he eased them down to reveal his well-endowed male essence.

"Oh my," Faith said in a helpless virginal tone. "Is all of that for me?"

"Nobody but you, woman," Gerard said, joining her on the bed and moving on top of her.

Faith embraced him and took pleasure in the warm feel of his flesh on hers and how their bodies melded together effortlessly. He wasted no time in bonding them with his rock-hard penis.

Letting out a sigh of contentment, Faith lowered her hands to her husband's bottom and gripped it while she set to writhing upon the throbbing fullness within her.

Gerard closed his eyes as though he were hypnotized by the rhythm of her hot, curvy body. Then he kissed and nibbled her lips and lowered his mouth to her nipples, which had turned to pebbles in the throes of their lovemaking. He licked and sucked on them, causing Faith to moan.

Consumed with rapture, Faith felt her blood sizzle and her body ebb and flow as though it were an ocean in the midst of a storm. She loved this man, and every time they came together this way, she made sure her body said as much as the words—"I love you."

Straining and wiggling in their sweetness, their bodies grew moister with sweat and wilder with each caress, with each touch and each wet, nibbling kiss they delivered to the erogenous zones they knew would heighten their passion.

As Gerard's expert touch sent her to higher levels of ecstasy, Faith's desire grew to explosive proportions she could no longer restrain. Soon her climax exploded, and she felt as though her soul had shattered into a million glowing stars. She cried out Gerard's name, sending him into a body-shuddering orgasm that made him groan her name as though he was in prayer.

In the afterglow of love, they lay drowned in a flood tide of the glory of their love and raw passion.

Breathing deeply and pulling Faith closer to him to nibble on her ear and layer her neck with soft kisses, Gerard said, "Was that dessert satisfying for you?"

She rolled toward him and sighed. "It was the best confection I've ever had." She leaned on his chest and gazed into his eyes. "And to think these goodies are my very own private stock." She kissed him deeply and sighed as though she was really tasting the heavy delight of sugar.

* * *

The next morning Gerard kissed and embraced Faith before leaving for his job at Bellamy National Bank. After she had seen him off, the telephone rang. It was her seventeen-year-old sister, Monica. Faith sat in the kitchen, chatting while she emptied bags of Halloween candy into a bowl for the evening's trick-or-treaters. She still had an hour before she was to leave the house to begin her day.

"Shouldn't you be on your way to school?" Faith asked, noting that if Monica wasn't at school in twenty minutes, she'd be late.

"I've got plenty of time. Besides, if I'm late, I have a note," Monica said in a blasé tone.

"I assume it's a forged one. Neither Daddy nor your mother expect you to get to school late, especially since they gave you that new car this past summer," Faith said, sipping on ginger tea to settle her upset stomach.

"Faith, I need you to be my sister and not my parent. I'm calling to ask you to talk to the folks for me concerning Ahmad," Monica said. "I think it's messed up they don't approve of me dating him."

In her mind's eye, Faith could picture her tall and lovely brown-complexioned sister, with her long raven hair parted in the middle, pouting as she expressed her displeasure over her social life. There was no doubt in Faith's mind that Monica was gazing into her compact, applying powder to her already glowing complexion, followed by lip gloss that she never went without in public.

"Sorry, Monica. I can't side with you on this one. I agree with them. Ahmad is cute in that bad-boy sort of way, but you deserve better. You deserve better than to be with someone who impresses me as being way too wrapped up in himself and his lofty hoop dreams."

"You're a snob, sis. You're only saying that because he doesn't come from the appropriate side of town," she sneered. "Then you know he has a baby. But he doesn't care about that girl. He tells me I'm the one he needs by his side. I have the class a rising athlete like him needs."

"He has you under a spell, doesn't he?" Faith stated impatiently. "Listen to me, Monica. Think about this situation. If this guy has used the mother of his child, it should tell you he has no regard for women. He might be all into you now, but I'm sure he'll break your heart too. Trust me on this one. Ahmad cares about no one but himself." Faith thought of the arrogant jock whom Monica had brought with her to Fabulous on several trips to the store.

Monica let out a gasp of frustration. "I can't. I have to go by Ahmad's feelings and the way I care for him. He loves me as much as I do him. He respects me too. And besides, that girl who had his baby tried to trap him because he's fine, and she knows he's going to the NBA and he'll have a fortune with all the attention he's getting from col-

23

leges and even professional teams. Don't you keep up with sports, Faith? Aren't you aware that Ahmad is considered one of the best players in the state? Agents and college recruiters are hanging around him and offering him all kinds of deals that could make him as huge as LeBron James."

"Love, huh? Pretty strong emotions for someone your age," Faith said, ignoring Monica's explanation.

"I'm not a child. I'll be eighteen in a few months. I know what and who I want. Please don't talk down to me," Monica snapped.

Faith was concerned. She had a feeling that this thing Monica had with Ahmad was on a physical level.

"Don't give me attitude, little sister," she chided. "I just don't want to see you getting hurt." Faith hesitated, then pushed on. "Monica, are you sleeping with Ahmad?"

Monica didn't respond, so Faith assumed she had hit on a sore spot. Her heart fell as she thought of her sister being sexually active at seventeen. Though Faith hadn't been a virgin when she married, she had waited until she was a few years older than Monica and she was in college. She had been emotionally ready for the experience and not pressured to have sex the way she feared Monica may have been.

Faith took a deep breath. "Do you think you're fascinated with Ahmad because of his chances of being a pro star?"

"Of course not," Monica snapped. "I like him because I think he's different from the other guys I've ever known. He's not immature or silly. Ahmad acts like a real man. Whenever I'm with him, I can feel the envy from all the other girls who wish they could be me."

"Have you ever considered that the reason Ahmad is so great to you is because our father is his basketball coach? Daddy has done a lot for that kid to get him to the point where he is with his sport. Daddy took him under his wing because he knows that boy's background, and he wants to see Ahmad break the cycle of poverty and abuse he's experienced as a foster child. And if you ask me, Ahmad's ego has gotten blown out of proportion from all the attention he's getting. He's beginning to forget those—especially Dad— who have helped him get his recognition. That know-it-all attitude he's taken with Dad alone should turn you off. Monica, you should be careful to whom you give your heart. At your age, you should meet other guys before you get too involved with a guy who has a kid and an overblown opinion of himself and his basketball skills."

"What a speech." Monica smacked her lips. "I don't want to know any other guys. Ahmad is good enough for me, regardless of what anyone else thinks."

Faith rolled her eyes. "Don't get an attitude, Monica. We need to discuss this more. I care about you, and I can see heartache ahead for you. I want you to avoid that, because he's not worth it, Monica. I don't want you to learn this the hard way. I believe you're fascinated with Ahmad because you know Dad and your mother don't want you close to him."

"You're wrong. It's time for everyone to stop trying to run my life. I'm capable of looking out for myself, Faith," she said defensively. "I thought for sure I could count on you to support me in my relationship, but I suppose you're too busy thinking of yourself and your perfect husband." Monica clicked off the phone.

Scowling at her sister's petulance, Faith hung up. Everything had become so dramatic to Monica since she had become smitten with Ahmad, Faith thought. Monica's emotional response convinced Faith even more that she was sexually active.

Their father, Rufus, and Monica's mother, Paula, weren't pleased with their daughter's interest in Ahmad and had discussed it with Faith. It was part of Rufus's responsibility as a teacher and a coach to take an interest in his players. However, it was distressing to Rufus that his baby daughter had chosen the one with the most issues to fall in love with. Though Ahmad had made an effort to straighten out his life, he still walked a thin line between crime and lawfulness, their father confided to Faith. Ahmad had been in and out of detention homes for shoplifting and even once for selling drugs when he was fifteen years old. Rufus, a high school physical education and health teacher who coached the boys' basketball team, had spoken up for Ahmad to the authorities to give him a second chance. Faith's father had done a good job of showing Ahmad his options to get out of the dark existence he had believed was his only destiny.

Draining the last of her tea, Faith thought of the doctor's appointment she had that day. She would make a point of talking to Monica again when she hoped she would be more reasonable. Faith went to shower so she would have enough time to drop by her clothing store, Fabulous, before heading to the doctor's office.

Sure enough, Monica was late for school, as Faith had predicted, and received after-school detention. She changed from one outfit to another, deciding which skintight designer jeans and long-sleeved shoulder-baring sweater she had chosen would make her look sexier and please Ahmad more. It wasn't until their lunch hour that Monica got a chance to catch up with her man. She caught sight of his long, lean brown frame and that fabulous smile of his. Ahmad stood in the corner of the lunchroom, surrounded by a group of girls who eyed him as though he were a pop idol. One girl, Joy—whom Monica considered her competition for Ahmad's heart, snuggled up beside him and placed her arm around his waist, then placed a kiss on his lips while her girls watched and laughed at Joy's open flirtation.

Monica's temper flared, and she rushed over to the group by Ahmad's side. She wedged her body between Joy's and Ahmad's. She eyed Joy and her friends contemptuously. Then she gave Ahmad a passionate kiss, even though he didn't return her action. Instead of an affectionate look, he gave her a baffled one. With a forced grin, he took hold of her hand and excused himself from the adoring girls. He led Monica out of the cafeteria and through doors that led to an empty stairwell. Once there, he took hold of her arm, squeezing angrily, and glowered at her.

"What the hell was that all about?" Ahmad asked, hovering over her. "How dare you embarrass me by trying to act like you own me. No one treats Ahmad like that." He gritted his teeth.

"But it's me you love," Monica said, fearing the look, and the tone in his voice. She was familiar with his rage. When he had grown impatient with her over her reluctance to become sexually intimate with him, he had threatened to dump her and to get with someone who would be more than willing to be a woman with him. Fearing she would lose him, Monica had surrendered her virginity. She'd tried not to regret her decision, because it had kept Ahmad happy and in her life.

"I'm getting tired of your possessiveness. You've got to chill, baby. I'm the man around this school. I won't have you making me look like a punk. If you can't accept that I'm the big man, then I'm going to have to cut you loose." He shoved Monica against the wall.

She hit it hard with her shoulder and let out a groan of pain. She began to cry and shiver from Ahmad's threat and cruelty.

"I love you, Ahmad," she whined, and began to sob loudly. "Why do you treat me this way?"

Ahmad rushed up to her. His face softened. "Shh . . . you don't want anyone to think I'm hurting you." He gathered her in his arms to hold her. "I didn't mean to hurt you. You—you just act crazy sometimes, Monica, and make me do things I regret."

She stared up at him, relieved that his mood had changed. "You get jealous when you see me talking with other guys, even my classmates. My world is you. I devote my time to you alone. I expect the same from you."

"It's different with me. I've got to be sociable with my fans. They're the ones who keep Ahmad from looking like a social outcast. I certainly don't want anything negative about my character to get back to the coaches who are interested in recruiting Ahmad. I need your support, baby. So you've got to stop acting like a little girl."

He cupped her chin and lavished her with one of his charming smiles that never failed to make her forgive him anything.

Her tears halted, and she gave him a smile and allowed him to kiss her to soothe the fear and confusion she'd felt moments earlier. They had the kind of love no one would ever understand, she thought in the midst of the sweetness from his lips.

"It looks as though you're pregnant," Dr. Lauren Wells informed Faith after her examination. "That was some honeymoon."

Faith grinned, remembering the week. "I have to admit it was wonderful. Just think, I'm going to be a mother before our first wedding anniversary."

Dr. Wells stood beside Faith and placed her hand on her shoulder. "You are truly blessed. You have a good man, your own business, and now you're going to have a beautiful child to add to your happiness."

Faith did feel fortunate. She had been ready for a family ever since her mother died of breast cancer when Faith was ten years old. Although her father had been as devastated as she had been, their relationship was troubled. Faith remembered how she had tried to be a comfort to her emotionally distant father by doing household chores and bringing home good grades. Though Faith's mother had told her how special she was to her father, he had not been very affectionate with her. Faith, rightly or wrongly, always sensed he wanted a son. Her father always spent time coaching or talking with the boys in her neighborhood. Rufus had left much of the raising of Faith to her mother.

When her mother fell ill with cancer, Faith was so lonely. She didn't like seeing her strong father looking lost and sad. He talked very little to Faith. It had been her mother who spent time talking and laughing with her and showing her how to do things around the house. Whenever they went out as a family, her father smiled and treated her mother and Faith as though they were his proud trophies. Yet after her mother died, Rufus never took time to find out Faith's feelings. There was only small talk between them.

Once Faith's mother was gone, several women had made an effort to slip into their lives. The women would invite him and Faith for home-cooked meals, or they'd give Rufus homemade desserts. When Faith turned twelve and started middle school, her father began to take more than a friendly interest in Paula Williams, a registered nurse, whom he had met through a mutual friend. They had a whirlwind romance and married before Faith's thirteenth birthday.

The doctor broke Faith's memories.

"Get dressed and come to my office so we can talk more," Dr. Wells said. "We'll figure out your expected due date. Congratulations, dear."

Brimming with joy, Faith sat on the end of the exam table. She thought of her dream of a son on her honeymoon. She was going to be a mother. How much better could her life become? she mused, touching her stomach.

She had mentioned to Gerard that she had an

appointment with her gynecologist, but she hadn't told him she suspected she was pregnant. She had been tempted to take a home pregnancy test, but decided against it. Faith wanted her condition to be verified by her physician before she breathed a word to Gerard.

She bounded off the table and reached for the cell phone to call Gerard at the bank. She was surprised when Mrs. Simpson, his secretary, told her Gerard had gone home for the day. Faith wondered if he was okay; he hadn't mentioned he would be taking a half day. A smile lifted the corners of her mouth. She would go home to tell him. Having him look her in the eyes when she made the announcement would be more priceless. She couldn't wait to see his expression.

CHAPTER THREE

On the drive home, Faith was bursting with exhilaration. She couldn't wait to see Gerard. When she turned on to their street a little after noon, she saw not only Gerard's car but also another one parked in front of their house. The last thing Faith wanted was to entertain when she had such awesome news.

Faith entered the house. She was thrown when she came upon the sight of a woman dressed in tight jeans, a too-tight T-shirt and high-heeled red pumps, standing over her husband. Faith offered a stunned smile to the woman, who glanced her way coolly.

"Hello," Faith said. "Gerard, I called the office, and Mrs. Simpson told me you'd left for the day." She came into the dining room and kissed her husband on the cheek.

Gerard jumped to his feet. "Faith, I'd like for you to meet Iris Burton Wynn."

The brown-complexioned woman with short, spiky hair gave Faith a withering look.

Faith's eyes widened at the name she recognized as her husband's ex-wife. What in the world would bring her to Bellamy for a visit at this time with her husband? Faith wondered.

"Hi," Faith managed.

Glancing at Gerard with a wry grin, Iris said with fake cheer, "Hey, girl." She waved her fingers, which had long acrylic nails painted a variety of bright colors.

Faith's heart stood still and her blood ran cold as she sensed trouble. Gerard had shared with Faith his unhappy experience of his first marriage to Iris. Iris had been a waitress in one of the diners that surrounded his college campus. Though she'd worked days as a waitress, she'd also danced in several rap videos. She had aspirations of being a legitimate actress one day. Gerard hadn't liked the idea of his curvy wife hanging out and partying with the famous rappers who she believed would help make her a star. Gerard had tried to be supportive of her dreams, but he felt disrespected when she had gone behind his back and posed nearly nude in several popular black men's magazines. He hadn't known about the pictures until his classmates had shown him his wife's sexy spreads. When he confronted Iris about what she had done, she had grown defensive and told him she refused to let him hold her back with his old-fashioned values from getting where she wanted to go. She wanted out of the boring life he had to offer. Gerard told Faith he had quickly discovered the only person Iris loved was herself.

However, since he had ended his relationship more than nine years earlier, Faith was puzzled by the woman's out-of-the-blue presence.

Gerard met his wife's inquisitive gaze with a tortured look, and rubbed the back of his neck. "Faith, um . . . I invited Iris to our home to discuss a private matter. She's come to town to convince me I'm the father of her eight-year-old son," he announced.

Faith gave him a halfhearted smile. "You've got to be kidding me." She lowered her eyes to see pictures of a child spread out on her dining room table. She returned her attention to her husband, placed her hands on her hips, and did her best to hide her shock. "What does she want from you?" Faith asked as though Iris wasn't in the room.

Iris sat in a dining room chair near where Gerard stood, and folded her arms beneath her ample breasts. The word "diva" was written in glitter on her T-shirt. She gave Faith a frigid stare.

"I don't want anything from you," she snapped. Then she focused on Gerard. "I came to deal with him."

A spasm of irritation crossed Faith's face, and she stepped closer to Iris. "If you're dealing with my husband, you're dealing with me. I won't have you disrespecting me in our home."

35

Beads of perspiration stood on Gerard's face, and he gave his wife an apologetic look.

Iris held up her hand as though to dismiss her. "The older my son has gotten, the more riddled with guilt I've become for withholding his presence from you. I'm not here to cause trouble. I just want to do what's right. When Gerard and I ended our thing, I couldn't get away from him fast enough. I wanted to travel and to get what gigs I could in the music videos, dancing or being the woman for the hottest rapper in the game. Just as things were taking off for me, I realized I was pregnant—right after we went our separate ways. You see, before those papers were filed, Gerard and I had a hellified argument over money, bills and personal belongings we'd bought as a couple, but somehow passion reared its head a final time during his last visit at my place." She leered at Faith. "I'm sure you've seen those movies with those clichéd arguments that end with couples falling into bed, rolling and tumbling, turned on by the passion of their differences. Good-bye sex is what produced our son." She laughed with delight.

Faith stared at this crude woman and imagined yanking her by her arm and shoving her out of her home and life.

Looking ashamed, Gerard frowned at his ex's tacky account. "Iris, where is your decorum?" he asked curtly.

"Oh, come on, Gerard. Put away your fancy

words with me." Iris shrugged and continued, "I was only explaining the situation that led us to making a kid." She turned to Faith and said, "It was only sex, Miss Lady. He and I had nothing more to do with each other after that final evening. He went his grumpy way, and I continued trying to get my career off the ground." She stood and stretched, as though the tale had worn her out. "Soon after, I learned I was pregnant. It had to have been that last tumble in the sack. I remember you not being concerned with precautions at that time."

Gerard listened with a sneer. "Why didn't you say something before now?"

Iris shrugged. "I didn't want to have any more dealings with you. I figured once you learned, you'd probably want to start acting as though you were my daddy as well as our child's. I tried to make it on my own, but I've come to realize a growing boy needs a father to show him how to grow into a man."

Faith began to applaud slowly. "What a performance. I don't believe you have your child's interest at heart. This visit is all about you. Admit it. You're tired of the responsibility of being a parent. I don't even know you well, but I can see you're the kind of woman who doesn't want to be tied down."

Iris gave Faith a scorching look. "You don't know me. So don't go making any assumptions about me."

"Stop," Gerard demanded, to take charge of the scene that was developing.

Iris rolled her eyes and dropped back into her seat. "Look, I'm here today so you and I can set things right for your son, Elijah."

Gerard sat down at the table and began looking over the pictures before him. "How thoughtful of you," he said in a sarcastic tone, eyeing the photos of the little boy she claimed was his.

Iris smirked. She took a picture from the collection and held it out to a sulking Faith. "Can't you see the resemblance?" she challenged. "Look at his eyes and the shape of his mouth. His features are just like Gerard's."

With Gerard staring at her, Faith accepted the picture and analyzed the facial features of the boy who had the same honey-colored eyes as her husband. His smile was even as warm as Gerard's, she observed. Faith's shoulders slumped as low as her spirits.

Gerard's brows knitted then. He glanced smugly at Iris. "Faith, Iris has been given a chance to do some modeling, and she has signed a contract to cohost a black celebrity entertainment news show. She's even gotten a small part in some movie."

Faith chortled. "Am I supposed to be impressed?" She glared at Iris. "I can imagine whatever modeling or acting she'll be doing will be triple-X."

Iris glowered at Faith. "There you go assuming

again. I told you, you don't know me. So just zip it, sistah."

"I'm no 'sistah' of yours. It's women like you who set bad examples for young women by jiggling and flashing their flesh for a dollar," Faith said fervently.

Gerard got up and went to his wife and slid his arm around her waist. "Calm down, please. I know this situation is as stressful for you as it is for me."

Faith stared away from them both.

"Iris has come here today to persuade me to assume the parental responsibility she's denied me all these years."

Faith said, "It's all about her. She's only thinking of her needs. That shirt she has on says it all. She thinks she is a diva, and now she wants to live like one at your expense."

Iris stared intensely at them. "Listen, I won't have you making me feel bad. This isn't all about me. It's about what's right for Elijah, so don't try to make me come off as thoughtless."

Faith's heart sank with despair, and a feeling of nausea consumed her, reminding her of why she had come home early. She realized her joyous news of their baby would fade after what Iris had inflicted on them. Exhaling to ease her tension, Faith sat in a chair near her husband, clutching the picture of Gerard's son.

"The child does resemble you, but that could be a coincidence," Faith said, ignoring Iris. "Surely you can't trust what she's told you after what you know of her lifestyle as a video girl," she said with derision. "I have an issue with her waiting a whole eight years to come forth. Get some valid proof before you even take on what she's suggesting." Tears glistened in Faith's eyes. "We're newlyweds, we've only begun our lives. We don't need this kind of drama."

Iris shot Faith a scorching look and placed her hand on her chest as if in anguish. "I know my timing is awful," she said in a controlled tone. "I can't blame you for hating me. Gerard mentioned you two had just returned from your honeymoon and moved into this lovely plush crib." She cleared her throat and her expression grew humble. "But Elijah needs a daddy—his daddy. I regret what I did. It was shortsighted, but I can't be both a father and a mother to my son." She gave Faith a pleading look. "I want nothing from your man for myself. This is strictly about Elijah."

"I really wish I could believe that," Faith snapped.

Looking chagrined, Gerard said, "Iris, I want proof that Elijah is really my blood. Plus you've told me this child has been clueless about me until now, so why would he want to live with me?"

"It'll work out. It has to," Iris said testily. "I've done what I can for him, and now it's your turn to get to know him."

Faith observed how Iris's eyes flashed with desperation.

Gerard turned pensive. He didn't know what

to do. He looked at Faith and could see clearly that she was dismayed. Then he examined more closely the pictures of the little boy whom Iris claimed was his, and he was floored. He was a good-looking child, and with what Iris told him about the boy's personality, he would be proud to have him as a son. He glanced toward Faith, who was studying him. He smiled weakly to cover the way the boy was already seeping into his heart. He'd never explained too deeply to Faith about his upbringing. She'd only known about his mother and how he had come to be reared by his grandmother. He had planned to give her more details now that they were married. How ironic, he thought, that Elijah might be coming into his life the way Gerard had shown up in his grandmother's.

Gerard had been barely six years old when his mother had left him. His mother was twenty-three, and she had promised to return when she was able to afford to give him a good home. Unfortunately he never saw her again. She'd left Virginia to live in New Jersey, and had gotten romantically involved with an abusive man who eventually took her life.

Gerard never forgot the day when he was eight years old and his grandmother had dressed him in white for his mother's funeral. He never forgot the rose he had been given to lay upon his mother's coffin. His grandmother told him his mother had gone to a better place, where there was no more heartache. He grew up clinging to pictures of her and listening to his grandmother speak of how smart and gorgeous his mother had been. His grandmother always painted a positive picture of his mother, who had been smart enough to be whatever she wanted, had she not fallen so deeply in love with all the wrong men.

Gerard tried not to dwell on the past. It was why he hadn't delved into this part of life as he should have with Faith. Yet all the memories resurfaced as he stared at Elijah's picture. Then he studied Iris, who looked much too anxious to rid herself of the all-consuming duties of a parent. He empathized with Elijah, whom he imagined had had a road of loneliness to travel with his mother, who was more obsessed with becoming a model or celebrity than with making a home for him. Though Gerard had been fortunate enough to have a grandmother who loved him deeply, he had yearned for the love of his mother and to know the father whom he'd never even met.

Iris spoke and ended the tense silence in the room. "If you want a paternity test, I'm more than willing to get it done. That way you and your bride won't feel as though I'm running a scam on you. I'm ready to get this settled as soon as possible."

Gerard blinked as though he were erasing the remembrances of his painful childhood. "Uh, yeah. I'm all for a test. I don't want to invest any time and emotion into someone who I might find out later . . . Well, Iris, you deceived me. You'd probably do the same thing if you were in my shoes," he said in a businesslike tone.

Faith spoke out. "How long are we expected to keep your child?"

Iris didn't look at her but instead at Gerard when she said, "I can't be specific. Since I've gotten an agent, I have enough work to keep me busy for several months at least."

"Several months," Faith exclaimed, jumping from her seat. She stared at Gerard and noticed the warning look in his eyes. She didn't know whether it was because of her volatile reaction or Iris's response. She walked in front of Iris to keep from being disregarded. "Certainly you have family or friends of your own somewhere to help you."

Iris's confident demeanor floundered briefly. "I don't have anybody, okay?" she said between clenched teeth. "Gerard is his father, and he should be glad I came to hand over his child he never knew about."

When Faith noticed how Gerard wouldn't look her way, she knew Iris had managed to strike an emotional chord in him. Faith felt a sickening sensation of despair. She could feel her near-perfect world crumbling. She couldn't help feeling that, again, she'd be on her own.

Gerard picked up one of the snapshots of Elijah and assessed it. "I will make arrangements for the paternity test," he announced in a controlled tone. He searched Faith's face for support.

Iris looked relieved. "Let's get it done quickly. Like I said, I have plans to make, places to go, and I want to make sure Elijah is taken care of." Iris reached in her handbag and handed Gerard a piece of paper with all the numbers where she could be reached while she stayed in Bellamy. With her head held high, Iris sauntered out of the dining room and exited the house, slamming the door.

Once she was gone, Gerard rubbed his temples. "I can't believe this."

Neither could she, Faith thought. Vexed, she wished her husband would give her a devilish grin and tell her this mess was a Halloween prank. They would have a big laugh over it; then she could tell him about the baby *she* was expecting. Frustrated, she looked at her husband, Gerard, who appeared to be overwhelmed.

CHAPTER FOUR

Tears spilled from the corners of Faith's eyes. "You shouldn't feel obligated to take on this child after the way that woman withheld this information for all these years."

Gerard rose from the table and gently grabbed hold of Faith's shoulders. "What's done is done. I'll take the test, then I'll do what I have to. If he's mine, I'm going to make every effort to have some kind of relationship with him."

Turning petulant, Faith stepped away from him and hugged herself. "You do what you have to, but don't expect me to have a hand in this parenting business. Iris doesn't deserve your support. She hasn't given any consideration to what is going on in your life, which is entwined with mine."

Distressed by his wife's withdrawal, Gerard had nothing to add to what had been said.

"What will become of our marriage if that child

comes to live with us?" Faith said with a moan. "Imagine what your coworkers will think of you when this eight-year-old shows up in our lives. I'd immediately think 'deadbeat dad,' just like I'm sure they will. Imagine the humiliation for me after our fairy-tale wedding. This is not fair. It's not fair to me at all."

Gerard's face twisted with irritation. "Enough! You're blowing this out of proportion."

Since Gerard had never raised his voice to her in anger, Faith's eyes widened. Already she saw their lives were changing. "No, I'm not," she answered slowly.

Seeing how hurt Faith was, Gerard's face softened. "I'm sorry. I didn't mean to shout. I'm stressed, sweetheart. Don't worry. I have more than enough love for you and this little boy, if he's mine."

Faith wanted to believe him, but her father promised the same thing when he had remarried and had another daughter with Paula. Unexpectedly, the new family had made her feel more insecure and inadequate in her father's eyes. After his second marriage, Faith felt as though she was an outsider in her own home, the home her father had allowed her stepmother to redecorate to suit her taste. Faith remembered the heartbreak as all the nice things Faith's mother had bought to make a cozy home for Faith and Rufus had been carted off to Goodwill.

Giving Gerard a dubious look, Faith wiped

away her tears. Her complexion was flushed from her anxiety. "More than enough love, huh? Yeah, I bet," she said coolly. She thought of her news about the baby. "But I'll never be the first to give you a son now," she said ruefully. She slunk out of the dining room.

The moment Faith left the room, she was hit by a wave of nausea that sent her dashing for the bathroom. Dropping to her knees in front of the commode, she vomited. After she was done, she broke out in a cold sweat. Standing on shaky legs, she assessed herself in the mirror. She tucked her freshly permed light brown shoulder-length hair behind her ears. Her heart-shaped face was streaked with tears, and her light brown eyes welled with more. The sparkle of joy and love that had been like an enhancing cosmetic had vanished. She was a vision of death warmed over, she mused, noticing the pallor of her honey complexion, and her eyes red-rimmed from crying. The beginning of motherhood was no joke, she thought. She placed a hand on her tummy, and a tremulous smile lifted the corners of her mouth.

Turning away from the mirror, Faith stumbled to the master bedroom. She fell upon the bed and began to weep loudly, releasing all the outrage and disappointment at the events that had spoiled her life. She knew deep in her heart that Gerard was the father of Iris's son. She wasn't ready to assume the role of being a stepmother, especially not to the child of someone as intolerable as Iris.

How could this happen to her again? She thought of how she had felt when Paula changed everything in her family. Paula took over, and her father had shown more appreciation for his new wife than he had for Faith's young efforts. Then Paula became pregnant, and Faith felt as though Rufus and Paula, with the anticipation of the new baby, formed an inner circle that she could never fully join. She thought of Monica, and how she had grown into liking being her big sister, although her younger sister had been spoiled and pampered from the moment she'd come into the world. Even though her father had been with Paula for over eighteen years, Faith still felt as though she had to fight for his consideration. Seeing him with his other family only made her wonder if her mother had been treated as regally as her dad treated Paula.

Faith hadn't been able to share her memories of her late mother, Clarice, with father's new family. In fact, Rufus had turned over the photo albums of his former life to her. It was as if he had closed the door to the happiness they'd known in those days. Now Gerard, the one man whom she loved and believed was hers alone, had come up with this hidden child from his nearly thirty-year-old ex-wife with delusions of grandeur. She acted as though she was a video princess and a sexy vixen of men's fantasies. Once again Faith felt as though she would be sharing the most important man in her life, and losing him. With that thought, Faith wore herself out crying until she drifted off to sleep.

She was awakened only when Gerard came in the room, took a seat on the bed beside her and tenderly stroked her hair away from her face with his warm, loving hand. "Are you okay?" he asked. "We've both been through a lot today. Believe me, I'm sorry for the way things have played out."

Sitting up in bed, Faith gave her husband a cold stare. She pushed away his hand as he attempted to rest it upon her face. "I can't believe this nightmare." She bounded from the bed and stood away from him with her arms folded. "I arrived home hoping to share some good news, but everything backfired on me."

Looking weary, he stared at her. "What did you want to tell me, sweetheart?"

"I had an appointment with Dr. Wells today. I'm five weeks pregnant," she announced.

The weary expression melted into softness. He took her hand and squeezed it. "That's wonderful!" he enthused, kissing her.

At that moment, Faith set aside her anguish. She relished his response and returned his kiss with a smile.

"What a day! I've learned I'm going to be the daddy of two kids."

Her dark mood immediately returned. Faith

pushed him away and walked to the dresser, staring at her puffy, sad face. She cringed and patted her face gently to rid it of its tired look.

"What did I say?" Gerard asked. He stepped behind her until he appeared in the mirror with her. His heart ached as he observed how the beauty of her confidence had slipped and been replaced with that of a little girl lost.

She whirled around and faced him with anger flashing in her eyes. "Surely you haven't claimed that other child already? The only child you should be concerned with today is the one you know is yours, the one I'm carrying."

Giving her a repentant look, Gerard said, "You're right. Today is our day. Let me take you out so we can celebrate the—the additions to our family."

"You mean the *addition*," Faith corrected him curtly.

Gerard blinked with incredulity. "Listen, we're both intelligent and mature adults. You saw those pictures of Elijah today. I'm not pleased with the way Iris handled this thing, but when I look at that child, I see myself. Of course I'm still going to have the paternity test done. It's a necessary formality for legal purposes, especially since I'm dealing with Iris."

His words made her feel tired. "Forget the celebration. I need to be alone. I'm going for a ride to clear my head." She stormed out of the room.

Gerard caught up to her and snagged her wrist,

pulling her against his long, lean, tough form. At that moment he looked very powerful, his chest broad and muscular. His brows and eyes showed determination. "Can't we be civil to each other over this matter? What has happened is unfortunate, but it hasn't changed my love for you. Faith, you have to remember the vows we made on our wedding day," he urged. Then his lips parted in a dazzling display of straight white teeth.

Faith wasn't fazed by his attempt to win her over. She didn't want to kiss and make up. She wasn't ready. Struggling to get away from him, she demanded, "Leave me alone. I've heard enough. Just let me go."

Gerard was unmoved by her tantrum. He held her tighter. "I'm not letting you go until I make you hear me out," he insisted. Frustrated, he exhaled loudly. He cupped her chin and lifted it so she could see his face. "During our wedding ceremony, we stood before a church full of people and vowed to love each other for better or worse. Well, we've come to the 'worse' much sooner than we expected. Surely you're not going to turn your back on me when I need you the most. If you love me as much as you say you do, you'd be supportive of me and of this boy who's coming into my life."

Her lashes swept down to her cheekbones, and tears spilled from the corners of Faith's eyes and trickled down her face to meet under her chin. She didn't like Gerard witnessing her display of weakness and was so ashamed that she pushed him away. "I do love you, Gerard, but I have our child to consider first. Get your test results back, then we'll discuss your being the boy's father. But right now, I don't want to deal with this." She fled from him to the front of the house and out the door.

Once she was inside her car, Faith rested her head on the steering wheel and sobbed. Then she started the car and drove away.

Faith rode around town for several hours, thinking. She knew her attitude was selfish, but she was only human. She resented the idea of having to share Gerard, but she could tell that he was bound and determined to be a father to Elijah. She knew she should admire him for his dedication and commitment, but her heart just wasn't in it. All she could do at this point was to hope for the best. With this thought in mind, she returned home and went to bed next to her sleeping husband.

It only took ten days for Gerard to get the results of his paternity test. He'd had his physician, Dr. Richter, take a sample of his DNA, and Elijah's pediatrician had sent the boy's to a lab that could give them the answer they needed.

Since Iris's visit, Faith and Gerard had lived their lives in tension and unnatural silence. The passion in the marriage had been nonexistent. Gerard had done nothing more than hold his wife's unyielding body at night. In the morning, they would share polite conversation concerning their work schedules and the activities or errands they had to attend to throughout the day.

After Dr. Richter called Gerard at the bank to tell him he had received the results, Gerard had called Faith and asked her to meet him at the doctor's office. She agreed to meet him, hoping that the tests would turn out negative.

Dr. Richter called the anxious couple into his office and read the results to them.

"Gerard, the test shows that you are Elijah Burton's father." Dr. Richter handed the results to Gerard and Faith to read.

Gerard stared at the official letter and handed it to his wife.

Staring at the letter, she masked her inner turmoil with a deceptive calmness. She returned it to Gerard and rose to leave.

"I have to get back to the store," she said, leaving Dr. Richter's office.

As she made her exit, she heard Gerard thanking the physician. Then he caught up with her in the reception room and tried to take hold of her hand. But she didn't want him to touch her. She glared at him, marched into the hallway, headed straight for the elevator and pushed the down button forcefully.

"I can imagine knowing the truth has stunned you. Now that there is no doubt, we can figure out what has to be done to include Elijah in our lives," he said. He stared at her and recognized the stubbornness on her face.

His words stabbed her heart. Couldn't he at least give her a chance to get used to the results? How could he expect her to begin making plans so readily? She felt he was being insensitive to her feelings. Though she tried to maintain her composure, her spirit was in chaos. She was glad when the elevator doors opened. She stepped into the empty car and moved to the corner of it.

Gerard followed and stood before her. "Faith, please say something."

"What is there left for me to say? You have a son. Congratulations, Gerard," she said, her voice rising hysterically.

The elevator came to a halt on the first floor and opened to several people in the lobby, waiting to get in.

Scowling at him, Faith stepped off the elevator and stalked away from Gerard toward the nearest exit to the parking lot and her car.

Gerard didn't go after her. He stood where he was and jammed his hands into the pockets of his slacks and gritted his teeth. His face was a mask of aggravation. He tilted his head back and let out a sigh of exasperation. Then he strode toward the exit and hurled himself through the door. Walking toward his car, he watched Faith zooming out of the parking lot and past him without looking his way. He stuck out his chin defiantly and cursed silently.

CHAPTER FIVE

After discovering that Elijah was indeed Gerard's son, Faith retreated into a shell of apathy and a life of work. Fabulous served as her saving grace over the next few days. Her trendy clothing store was the realization of a high school dream. Faith had always had an interest in fashion. In high school, she hadn't had the money to spend on the designer clothes she'd liked in fashion magazines and on her favorite music or movie idols. Yet she had an impressive gift for emulating the stylish looks on a budget. As a college student with a major in fashion and a minor in business, Faith kept notebooks with plans for a store that would sell inexpensive, tasteful, yet stylish clothes to teens and women in their twenties. Being able to own and operate a store in the new mall—Bellamy Square—had been her proudest achievement. From the grand opening to the present, Fabulous had been a success. In fact, business was so great that she was considering opening another store in one of the older malls nearby in Virginia Beach. Of course, she would begin this project after the birth of her baby.

With Elijah's impending arrival, Faith turned to running Fabulous as a refuge. She was grateful for her Friday-evening committee meeting concerning the fund-raiser the next day of Bellamy Square Mall for the Morning Has Broken Foundation. There she had a chance to see her friends Sydney Jackson and Nicole Brickle and could not only work with them, but also share the personal problem she had only had time to tell them of during phone conversations.

Arriving at Nicole's home, Faith found her friends in the midst of boxes of T-shirts and other items they expected to sell. The profits from this particular sale were to help furnish a halfway house for battered women and former drug addicts.

The Morning Has Broken Foundation had claim to a two-story building that had once served as a fire station. It had been chosen because it could house at least twenty-five women comfortably. However, they needed money for renovations and furnishings. But the money they planned to raise from a seventy-five-dollar-per-person Black and Silver–themed ball, along with donations from sororities, fraternities, and other philanthropic organizations and donors, was expected to take care of the restoration of the building.

That evening the women's main focus was the items at the kiosk they planned to sell in order to pay for the furnishings they needed. They went over the schedule of the volunteers who would work two-hour shifts and then sorted through their stock to make sure it was presentable.

"Girl, I'm so glad you made it out. With you running your business and being a newlywed with a major challenge to contend with, we wouldn't have been mad at you for backing out." Nicole offered a comforting smile to Faith. "I was jealous of you when I first saw you when you got back from your honeymoon. It was evident that marriage was agreeing with you. You were glowing." Nicole put some items into a box. "It's a shame that hussy from the past showed up, ruining everything between you and Gerard. I bet you never imagined yourself in the role of stepmother. If you need any legal advice, I'm available," she offered. She shared a legal practice with her husband, Donald. The two were now trying to start a family.

Sydney, a former surgical nurse, said, "The situation is surreal. I mean, Gerard would be the last person I'd think something like this would happen to. Talk about drama and I can see that it's wearing on you by the sad look in your eyes. You and Gerard haven't had a chance to live in bliss the way newlyweds should. You know I feel that a couple should have time to really get to know one another as husband and wife before a child strange to both of you enters the picture." Sydney had been married to an orthopedic surgeon for six years, and had a five-year-old daughter and a three-year-old son. "With the presence of an eight-year-old boy, you're going to have to be an extrastrong sister."

Faith listened while replacing a stack of large-sized T-shirts in a box. Then she looked at her friends and announced, "I'm pregnant. I went to Dr. Wells and had it confirmed. Isn't that just wonderful?" Her voice quavered.

Sydney and Nicole exchanged concerned looks. Both of them left their tasks and went to Faith to embrace her and congratulate her.

"Congratulations, Faith. That's great news for you," Sydney said, seeing her friend's eyes misting. She placed her arm around her shoulder.

Nicole took Faith's hand. "Yes, it is. Don't worry, I'm sure everything is going to be fine. She patted Faith's tummy and grinned. "You've got yourself and this baby of yours to consider."

Suddenly Faith let go her tears and sobbed.

"Oh girl, c'mon. Things are going to get better." Sydney leaned toward and handed her some tissues. "I can imagine you're overwhelmed with the idea of having two children. But you'll adjust. I'll be around to give you pointers. I'm only a phone call away."

"They sure can't get any worse," Nicole said before quickly adding, "One positive thing you've got going for your marriage is that you have a good and decent man in Gerard, who impresses me as a man born to be a father."

Sighing to regain her composure, Faith smiled weakly. "I feel so foolish. I'm going to be okay," she said, trying to reassure her friends. "I just feel weighed down with everything in my personal life happening so fast."

"There's no doubt your plate is full," Nicole said. "You're going to get through this. I know you will."

Faith forced a grin, still not knowing how she was going to manage. "Oh well, we'll see. Enough about me and my problems. We have women who have some truly serious issues who are depending on Morning Has Broken for assistance in their bruised lives." Faith cleared her throat, smiled, picked up her leather-bound notebook and clicked her ballpoint pen.

She caught Nicole and Sydney exchanging suspicious glances. She could see that she hadn't fooled them with her facade, but they did not comment.

Sitting up straight in her seat, Faith asked, "Uh—have you two given any thought to what you plan to wear to the ball? You've got to get it together. It's scheduled for New Year's Eve," Faith reminded them. "With a little more work, it will go over big and give us a chance to hit up the professionals we know for some generous donations. Our goal is to have that halfway house renovated, furnished and ready to use by spring. We want to make sure that we will be able to stock it not only with furniture, but also with computers, books and anything else the women may need to make new starts in their lives," she said with delight. "Hopefully we'll be able to get other organizations to donate additional items to the Foundation."

Nicole nodded. "I'm looking forward to the ball. Not only because it's already buzzed as the social event of the season, but also because it'll give me a chance to get dolled up and to get my husband into something other than khakis and a denim shirt to take me out. He hasn't been in a tux since we got married."

"I second that," Sydney said. "I want to have that bubbly prom feeling again." She burst out laughing. "I have my eye on two gowns. One is a sexy black number and the other a two-piece glittery silver outfit."

"Oh girl, I have my sights set on a slinky beige sheath with a split up the front," Nicole said.

Amused, Faith couldn't resist saying, "Ladies, aren't we forgetting the significance of this fundraiser? It isn't about us and our dresses. It's about the needy who'll benefit from this project."

Both Sydney's and Nicole's faces lit with angelic smiles.

"Of course we know this. But why can't we have a good time doing it, too?" Sydney asked. "I'm sure you won't have trouble finding anything to wear. I can imagine you'll probably order something from out of town that will put us all to shame."

Nicole picked up her notebook and opened it. "Faith, you know you're as into this ball as we are."

"Okay, I have ordered a baby-blue–colored satin gown with no straps," Faith admitted with a giggle. "I hope I won't have to have it altered due to my pregnancy."

"You're trim, so you probably won't show until later on in your pregnancy," Sidney said in a reassuring tone.

"I know you're going to be gorgeous. You and Gerard will be making goo-goo eyes, and everyone will yearn to be newlyweds in love like you two are."

Smiling politely, Faith cleared her throat to quell the swell of emotion that lumped there. "Once we get that building done, we can move our business office for the foundation there as well," Faith said, changing the subject.

Sydney thought out loud. "That'll be so convenient. I'd like for the place to have a more feminine and cozy ambience this time. After all, we're dealing with women who have been through a lot. They deserve all the coddling and encouragement we can offer them."

As Nicole resumed her work, she said, "I'm proud of our sorority, Alpha Kappa Alpha, and the way a lot of women from our chapter have volunteered their services to us for this project. The other committees have been working hard on this along with us too. I think we have every right to pat ourselves on the back for what we began." Nicole bragged. "And if I say so myself, we've done a good job with what we've been assigned to do. Eva Carey and her group are working hard to set the charity ball into motion. I'm sure she's going to make that a night to remember, with her eye for details, style and class."

"We sure have," Faith said, feeling her spirits lift a bit with her idea. "People think of black sororities as only a bunch of snooty professional women who are self-absorbed princesses. I'm most proud of what we've done with the women who have looked to us for help."

"I'm glad you got me involved in this program," Sydney said to Faith, touching her hand. "At first I was skeptical about getting involved in the battered women's program. Not experiencing the kind of violence and disrespect these women have taken from men, I didn't think I would have anything in common with them. But I have to admit that working with them all this time has made me a better person. It takes a lot of courage for these women to begin again and to return to their families and be the strong, self-respecting women they were born to be."

Faith nodded her agreement. "You know, as women, we have a tendency to be too cool toward one another. When things aren't too busy in the mall, I observe the way women react to one another. They stare like enemies or else walk past as though everyone is invisible. Unfortunately I see this in a lot of us young black sisters. We act as though a smile or a simple hello would cost us a fortune."

"It has to do with men, girl. It's always about men, isn't it?" Nicole pointed out. "When I was younger and a bit insecure, there were very few girls who I let in my life. I didn't want anyone around who might be temptation for the guys I dated before I met my husband, Donald."

Sydney laughed. "I felt the same way. It has to do with men and our insecurities about ourselves. We see a sister dressed in a great outfit or who is just blessed to be gorgeous, and immediately we assume she thinks she's better than us."

"You know I had to deal with that in high school and college," Faith admitted. "People assumed I spent a lot of money on clothes and assumed I thought I was better. But, that wasn't the case. Little did they know that I had no more money to spend on clothes than the next girl. Fortunately I have always been able to imitate the styles and trends I've seen in magazines, but on a budget."

Nicole grinned. "Though I wasn't that friendly with you from high school, I used to think you were a funky dresser. But you used to set the fashion trends at Hampton U," she said, thinking of their college days.

"I was glad you were our friend," Sydney added. "Nicole and I had our own personal stylist, thanks to you. At first I didn't like it when you were assigned to Nicole's room and mine, since the dorms were overcrowded as it was. She and I used to think you were snobbish, but we soon learned you were only shy." Sydney added with a smile, "And choosy about who you let in your life. I'd never imagined that we'd come home from school with a lasting friendship."

Thoughtfully, Faith ran her fingers through her hair. "Speaking of misunderstood, I was thinking Morning Has Broken should consider mentoring a group of black teen girls from various economic backgrounds. What about having a two-week session in the summer where we have discussion groups on various subjects from sex to self-esteem issues for these girls? Of course, it will be important for us to have specialists in each area to talk with them. We have plenty of professionals who work with Morning Has Broken who will be more than willing to assist. Then we can bring in fashion and makeup tips for them for fun." Her eyes lit up with the excitement of her idea.

"It sounds wonderful," Sydney said.

"I believe so," Faith said, noticing how Nicole's expression showed agreement. "I have some ideas in mind that will help to bond the girls and keep them from being intimidated by one another. I feel they'll learn to be more thoughtful and caring toward one another. Don't you think?"

Sydney said, "Most definitely. I'd love for my

Imani to have something like that when she's older."

"I say let's put it motion as soon as we deal with this charity ball," Nicole said.

"I'm glad you guys like the idea. I'll begin to write up a proposal so we can present it to the other members at our next meeting," Faith said.

"Faith, isn't this a bit too much for you to take on right now? I mean, you have yourself, a baby to take care of and a husband too," Sydney said. "You need TLC more than ever with all you're going through."

"I heard that." Faith laughed halfheartedly. "I'm going to be there for my husband." Faith's heart grew heavy, and she felt like a hypocrite. Gerard was faced with a dilemma, and she had made it clear she wanted no hand in it. What would everyone say if they knew how bitter she was over the situation? After all her talk of sisterhood, would Nicole and Sydney think her a fake?

Yawning, Nicole closed her notebook. "It's getting late. Let's call it a night. We've done all we need to do for our weekend fund-raiser. How about some snacks and a cool drink to relax from all the work we've done for today?"

"I'd like that," Faith said. She welcomed the chance to visit longer. She would much rather be there than have to head home and think of how Elijah had been forced upon her.

* * *

Gerard was dismayed when he called Faith at Fabulous and learned she wouldn't be home until later. He felt she had been avoiding him because of the revelation about his son. He missed the sound of her laughter and the easy conversation they had shared. Most important, he had missed the hot passion and the way his sophisticated wife turned into a vixen in their bedroom. All of that was gone since the paternity results confirmed him as the father to Iris's son.

Refusing to spend another evening alone, Gerard called Alex. He needed to speak confidentially to his best friend. Alex had to work late and told Gerard to meet him at his favorite steak-and-seafood restaurant in the downtown district, where he was planning to grab a bite to eat instead of going to his grandparents' soul food restaurant for dinner.

The restaurant, known for its juicy and tender steaks and delectable seafood, brimmed with its regular customers, Gerard observed. He spoke to several of his friends whom he hadn't seen since he had become a married man. The waitress, who knew him by name, informed him that Alex had not arrived yet. She showed Gerard to a booth near the window. Gerard ordered a beer and a shrimp-and-French-fry platter to satisfy his appetite.

While he waited for his food, Alex arrived, dressed in a suit with his tie dangling around his neck. Gazing admiringly at him, the waitress smiled broadly and pointed to where Gerard was seated. Alex whispered something to her, and she let out a girlish giggle.

Alex folded his long form in the seat across from Gerard. "Hey man, how's it going?"

Gerard sipped his beer. "I see you're still the favorite customer here."

"Don't hate, brother. This is like a second home to me. These ladies take care of me when I come here for cold beer and to hang out and watch the game on sports night." He signaled for a waitress and ordered a pitcher of beer. Alex smiled at the young bronze-skinned woman, who quickly bought the beer for him. She handed Alex a menu and said she would return shortly for his order.

"What are doing hangin' with me? I thought you'd be enjoying a home-cooked meal and cuddling with your wife." He glanced over the menu.

"That's what I should be doing, but ever since we've gotten the proof that Elijah's mine, it has grown even cooler at home. Faith is avoiding me by claiming to work late or having some kind of meeting or other to attend," Gerard admitted. Stress lines formed on his brow.

Alex settled back in his seat and rubbed his chin. "Oh man, you're in it deep."

"Tell me about it. I feel as though I'm caught up in a soap opera."

"That says it all. A new wife, a secret kid and a baby on the way with your bride—that clearly spells trouble," Alex said.

The waitress appeared to take Alex's order of a

medium-rare steak, salad and baked potato, and left.

"I don't know which way to turn, man. Iris will be bringing Elijah to us soon. She's anxious to follow through on these acting and modeling gigs she has." He turned sullen. "I can't imagine how I'm going to bond with this child who is going to look at me as though I'm a stranger. I bet he's wondering where I've been all his life and why I haven't taken the time to get to know him."

"The only thing for you to do is to take it one day at a time, man," Alex suggested. He shook his head sympathetically. "One minute you're a man who is madly in love with his wife, and the next minute you're a father with two kids and a wife who feels betrayed."

"Faith is crushed," Gerard admitted. "I can't really blame her for the way she's been treating me. I'm going to give her some time and space to get used to all of this. I've made an effort to appease her. But no matter what I say or do, she treats me like I'm a villain who was out to hurt her intentionally."

"Iris has always been selfish," Alex said. "You know that yourself from being in that quickie marriage with her. Iris is running away from her responsibility, man. She must think she's going to be the next hot diva. But if you ask me, she wants her freedom so she can hook up with some hip-hop star with deep pockets. She wants to live large."

He laughed sarcastically. "I hope all of this doesn't ruin the great thing you have with Faith. It would be a sin if that happened."

The waitress appeared with Alex's food and began to chat with him.

Gerard tuned them out and began to finish his beer. He stared out the window of the restaurant and watched the rain that had begun to fall. He worried how he was going to stretch himself and take care of his blended family.

CHAPTER SIX

The night before the event at the mall, Faith had stayed out until after midnight with her friends to finalize things on their project. Afterwards, she had taken the girls to a nearby restaurant, on her, for a light snack and drinks to avoid coming home and facing Gerard. She didn't want to hear of his plans for welcoming Elijah into their home. She knew he had been busy turning one of their four bedrooms into a personalized domain for his eight-year-son. She hadn't had a hand in it. She said she was too busy with her own life to assist him with whatever it was he doing.

When she reached home, she was grateful the house was quiet. She quietly made her way to their bedroom and found Gerard sound asleep with the television on. Though she was tired from her long day, she wasn't ready to join Gerard in bed and have him snuggle up to her—not with her confused feelings.

71

She went into their family room and stretched out on the sofa, turned on the television and was fortunate enough to catch the beginning of her favorite movie, *Love Jones*. Lying in the darkness, she watched the first sexy scene, where the two lovers hadn't been able to resist the lust they'd felt on their very first date. She envied the couple's lack of inhibitions and related to the hot passion they'd shared. She and Gerard had all of that and more until the child thing. Listening to the morning-after conversation of the characters in the movie, Faith sighed and closed her eyes to rest them. . . .

Suddenly Gerard appeared in the doorway of the room. She glanced in his direction and noticed how sexy he looked in only his pajama bottoms. His chest glistened as though he had used baby oil. His well-toned body looked enticing, she thought, wiping away the sleep in her eyes.

"Where have you been? I was worried about you. I've called around trying to track you down."

"I was with my committee, making sure everything was set for tomorrow," she answered.

Gerard strolled over to where she lay, and sat down on the edge of the sofa. He caressed the side of her face in a slow, tender manner. "Don't keep shutting me out, baby. I love you." His voice was full of heart-wrenching emotion. He took hold of her shoulders and lifted her into a sitting position to embrace her.

Faith couldn't resist the feel of his bare chest or of his touch. She surrendered to his embrace and began to sob upon his broad shoulder. Feeling his distress, she was appreciative and welcomed the kisses he lavished on the side of her face and then on her lips. The sweetness of his kisses warmed her body.

"You're still my wife, and you're going to be the mother of our child. We have so much ahead with two kids to love. It's time for us to be the way we were—lovers, friends and partners," he murmured into her ear.

With all the intensity he had switched on, she became uneasy. Faith pushed away from him. She still didn't want someone else's child intruding on the world she had orchestrated for herself and Gerard out of love. She bounded from the sofa and fled into their bedroom, where Gerard quickly followed. There she proceeded to undress. All the while, she could feel his eyes on her as she stripped down to her bra and panties, revealing her perfect trim, yet curvy, form.

Feeling his eyes burning into her, she glanced at him to see his brown face glowing with a lustful smile. He strolled up to her and placed his hand on her middle, where he knew his seed grew within her. Giving him a half smile, she removed his hand, walked away from him and headed for the bathroom for a shower. Standing beneath the steamy spray, she turned to see Gerard observing her. He shucked off his pajama bottoms and stepped nude into the stall with her.

She gave him an irritated look that soon faded as he enfolded her in his arms and pulled her against his strong body to claim her lips with an eager kiss. He placed tiny kisses on the side of her face and down her neck.

Relenting, she looped her arms around his neck and relished the feel of his healthy arousal that pressed against her womanly essence. She grew weaker as his lips returned to hers and they began to engage in a tongue-tangling kiss that made her crave him more.

Drenched from the shower, Faith pressed her breasts so close against his chest that she could feel his heart thumping against her own. Soon she felt his hands sliding up and down the curves of her body while he parted her lips with his tongue. Probing the inside of her mouth, her husband's hot breath coupled with his crushing kiss reminded her of how much she loved him and needed him. Brushing her feminine essence against him, she was consumed with overwhelming desire.

As she grew nearly breathless, Gerard whirled her around and pulled her flush against him, locking her snugly with his strong arm. He nibbled her neck and fondled first one breast, then the other. Thumbing each nipple into a pouty peak, he whispered erotic wishes while he lowered his hand and sought the dewy wetness of her love cove.

Feeling his insistent fingers within her, Faith

moaned softly and swirled her hips to the thrills he delivered so skillfully. Restless to be united with him, she turned to face him.

Giving her a look of fiery desire, he lowered her to the spacious floor of the shower and moved on top of her, penetrating her with a confident thrust.

Drugged and hazy from his ardent passion, Faith wrapped her legs around his hips and held on to his broad shoulders, setting a wondrous pace to their love journey. With the water pelting them, Faith closed her eyes and pretended they were back on their Jamaican honeymoon, making love in the island rain. Her thoughts made their intimacy sweeter. She clutched him around the waist and lifted her hips upward to him, whimpering with delight from each of his thrusts.

Gerard swiped his tongue over and around each of her globes before bracing his hands under her hips. He glided in and out of her, groaning from the hot pleasure they'd stoked.

The rapturous emotions made Faith's heart glow and her spirits soar. Soon she couldn't restrain herself from the glory of their oneness. Letting out a cry of satisfaction, she quivered in rapture, reaching an astounding climax. . . .

Faith awakened to the sound of screaming from the television. She'd missed the rest of her romantic movie, and her television was in the midst of a gory horror tale. Faith rolled to her side and breathed deeply to calm the racing of her heart from her passionate dream. Her center throbbed and was moist, as though she had been loved by her husband. But it had only been a fantasy.

She dragged herself off the sofa and decided to spend what was left of the night in the comfort of her bed.

Faith was up bright and early the morning of the fund-raiser. By the time Gerard had risen, Faith had eaten breakfast and was busy preparing a healthy lunch and snacks that would satisfy and nourish her new hearty appetite.

When Gerard entered the kitchen wearing only his pajama bottoms and looking as sexy as he had in that dream of hers, she experienced a shiver of déjà vu she hoped he hadn't noticed.

"Good morning," he said, giving his wife a tentative glance. "Today is an extra long day for you, right? Is there anything I can help you with?"

Without looking at him, she answered, "Thanks, but I'm fine." She zipped her thermal lunch bag.

"There's bound to be something for me to do," Gerard insisted lightly. "You're going to be running Fabulous and then pulling a shift at the fund-raiser booth. You may be tired because of the pregnancy. I'm available for whatever chore you may have for me." He stood near his wife, who began to fan through the morning paper while standing at the counter sipping orange juice.

She gave him a polite smile. "Get some of your friends and their wives or girlfriends to stop by the Morning Has Broken booth to support us. That would be a big help."

"I've done that already. I've spoken to the tellers and anyone else who would listen about Morning Has Broken. Quite a few people plan on stopping by," he assured her.

"How thoughtful," she said mindlessly, reading the paper.

Gerard stood at the fridge and poured himself some juice. "You stayed up late last night. I found you sound asleep on the sofa, but you were resting so peacefully that I didn't bother you."

She turned the pages in the paper and said, "I had a business meeting with the girls, and we went out after that for a snack. I stayed up watched television for a while and fell asleep." She shrugged. "This pregnancy is really draining my energy."

Gerard set aside his glass of juice and stood before her, placing his hands on her waist. "I know the results of the test floored you. No matter what, I'm still your husband, and I'm going to be a good father to our baby too."

Meeting his sincere gaze, Faith wasn't ready to relent. She resented how willing he was to let Elijah into their lives. She still felt as though he was betraying her and their marriage.

When Faith didn't say anything, Gerard urged her to look at him by touching her face. "Am I on punishment? Is that why you lay in our bed as far away from me as you can, to avoid me and my touch?"

Glancing at her watch and noticing it was nearly nine o'clock, Faith stepped away from him. "I don't know what to do or how to act," she admitted quietly. "This doesn't feel right."

"It can be. All you have to do is accept it and trust my love," he urged her.

Shrugging and pinching her lips together, she picked up her lunch bag and grabbed her coat. "Since I'll be working with the Foundation today, I'll be leaving the store early," she said, not acknowledging what he had said. "Come to the mall later. I'm sure there'll be something for you to do. I'm sure you'll see plenty of people you can corral our way." She offered him a sad smile.

"Okay, will do," he said, following her out the kitchen and into the garage. "Can I at least get a kiss or a hug? You haven't let me taste you or hold you for the last few days."

Staring into his eyes, she opened her arms.

He filled them and pulled her to him and gave her a lingering kiss.

She didn't resist him. Though she didn't show it, his kiss sang through her veins. Breaking away from him, she climbed into her car. "Got to go. See you later," she said. She put the car in reverse and backed slowly out the garage with Gerard watching her.

Pulling away from the house and toward the highway, Faith sighed to relieve the desire Gerard aroused in her. His willingness to bring Elijah into their home bought out a selfish side in Faith. She hoped her husband would see that he could risk losing her and had created problems in their marriage that didn't have to be. Maybe he would come to his senses and point-blank tell Iris she would have to make other arrangements for their son. Faith could withstand an occasional visit from Elijah so Gerard could become a part of his life, but the thought of him moving in with them during such a crucial time was too much for her. As she rolled the car into her space outside the mall, her ringing cell phone bought her out of her thoughts. Answering it, she was greeted by Monica's voice.

"I need to come by your store. I'm going to need something great to wear for homecoming," Monica said. "Ahmad and I will be by sometime today."

"Give me, give me," Faith teased. "I'd like to hear you show you care about me and ask how I'm doing. You know I'm sensitive since I'm about to become a mother."

"Sorry. How's the new mommy- and stepmom-to-be?" Monica asked.

"I'm fine and the baby is fine, but I'm not ready to be a stepmom. But that's a whole other matter that you're too young to discuss with me."

Monica sighed with exasperation. "I'm so tired of everyone treating me like a child. I'm nearly eighteen years old. I'm glad Ahmad doesn't think of me as a child."

"Please, spare me from Ahmad's opinion. You're far from being a wise woman."

"Ha ha," Monica said, clearly not amused by her sister's patronizing tone. "What time would be good for me to come by your hole in the wall so you can help me pick out a fierce dress?"

"Today is definitely not the day. With the holidays approaching, we have been really busy. Then I have that Morning Has Broken fund-raiser to supervise and work at for part of the day. It would be nice for you to help out, kid, instead of spending all your free time with Ahmad," Faith hinted. "Not only will you be doing a good deed, but you'll be doing the kind of community service that will look good on your college applications."

"I don't have time for that today. But the next time you have a thing, I'll help out. Ahmad and I have plans for later," Monica explained.

"What could be more important than being with your Ahmad?" Faith asked, thinking how her sister was wasting her time with that guy. "You're too wrapped up in pleasing that guy. Lately your whole world has become him. What do you do for yourself anymore?" Faith chided.

"You're beginning to sound like Mom and Dad," Monica said. "They're always fussing over the time I spend with Ahmad. I wish everyone would back off of me and let me live my life."

"Listen to you," Faith said with shock. "Ahmad is changing your attitude. The Monica I knew wouldn't be offended by her family taking an interest in her life."

Monica let out a sigh of exasperation. "Can I or can't I come to get something out of Fabulous?"

Faith didn't like her attitude and was tempted to hang up on Monica. However, she feared her younger sister shutting her out of her life. This relationship Monica had with Ahmad worried her. "Come around noon and bring a better attitude," Faith ordered.

Faith was pleased with the steady business at her store and in the mall that November day. Faith valued Tasha Nelson, who had been working at Fabulous for the last year. She was one of the success stories from the Morning Has Broken Foundation. A few years before, Tasha had been on the streets, using drugs. She had fallen into addiction because of a man she'd loved led her to drugs and then turned abusive. Once Tasha had gotten strung out on drugs, the dealer boyfriend got arrested for two murders and for possessing and distributing heroin. He'd received two life sentences for his crimes.

Thirty-five-year-old Tasha had been referred to the Morning Has Broken Foundation and their halfway house. Slowly, she had managed to get her life straight. Looking at the glowing chestnut face of a woman with a great sense of humor, no one would have guessed the struggles she had been through. Faith trusted Tasha, as her assistant, to run the store and to keep her four young employees in line.

During a lull in business, Tasha gave Faith a concerned look. "You don't look like you're feeling like all that today. Are you experiencing mood swings already with your pregnancy?"

Leaning against a dress rack, Faith gave her a halfhearted smile. She had shared the news of her pregnancy with Tasha because she knew she was going to have to rely on her support more at the store.

"I think my busy schedule doesn't agree with this baby I'm carrying," Faith smiled sadly. "And yes, I've been riding an emotional roller coaster."

"You'll be fine. You're a healthy woman," Tasha assured her. "You've got me and the staff to help you with whatever needs to be done here. We sisters will stick together for you." She winked at her.

Faith obliged her with a warm smile. "I want this baby, but now that it's a reality, I'm scared. I wonder if I'll be a good parent."

"Every woman goes through your kind of anxiety. You just have first-time nerves. As long as you love that baby and give it all the love you feel, you'll do just fine," Tasha said. "You're going to be a good mama."

Faith sighed. "You make it sound easy."

"It can be wonderful, but it's also the hardest

job you'll ever have. I have two preteens that keep me on my toes still," Tasha said.

Since Tasha had gotten her life together, she had met a churchgoing man and married him. With his love and support, she'd been able to reclaim the daughters whom her mother had raised when she'd been on the streets.

"My hat is off to you," Faith said. "Your girls are well mannered, and they're doing well in school, too. You and your husband have every right to be proud of them."

"I have to give my mother credit for watching out for them when I wasn't able. I had to earn their trust and love, but thank goodness we've bonded good. When I got married, things were rough for a while. My kids didn't know whether my husband was going to turn into the kind of monster I used to waste my life on. But Russell—being the fine man he is—has won them over. He shows his love and respect. Russell was more concerned with who I had become than with the lost soul I'd been for so many years." She grew quiet and looked overcome with emotion. "I suppose I owe my blessed life to Morning Has Broken. With the help from counselors and the assistance from the foundation, I was able to become the kind of woman my daughters could respect and let back into their lives."

Faith went to her and patted her hand. "I'm so happy for you. You have to take credit for all the courage and determination it took for you to turn it around. You do realize that we do have women who come through the foundation but aren't as successful as you."

Before they could further their conversation, the store had a fresh crop of customers who required their attention. Faith was assisting a teen in selecting her size of jeans from the new stock she'd recently received, when she spotted Monica sulking into the store, her ear to her cell phone. When Faith heard her call out Ahmad's name, she sensed there was tension between the two.

Approaching Monica, Faith noticed how her sister winced as she glanced at the phone before slapping it shut. Seeing Faith, she gave her a crooked grin.

"I was beginning to wonder if Ahmad had changed your mind about coming here today," Faith said.

"Uh—Ahmad had other plans. He got tired of waiting for me. I've been at the beauty parlor most of the morning getting a touch-up on my perm." Monica ran her fingers through her shiny long hair. Then she strutted over to a section with colorful dresses that would be appropriate for a homecoming dance. "I really like these styles," she said, pulling out her choices in size seven. "I'm going to try these on." Monica marched to the back of the store to the dressing rooms.

Returning to the counter, Faith began to help Tasha ring up the waiting customers.

"Your sister is on a mission, I see," Tasha said.

"Yeah, a mission to break me financially," Faith said. "She came in for a dress, but I bet she's going to leave here with more once she sees the new stock." She shook her head and laughed softly.

Once the lines had faded, Faith went to help her sister. It had been nearly fifteen minutes since Monica had disappeared in the dressing room without surfacing for Faith's opinion.

"Hey, how are you making out in there?" Faith called to Monica.

"I'm okay. I'll be out in a minute," Monica said in a teary voice.

Concerned, Faith opened the door to find Monica sitting on a bench dressed in her underwear. She clutched her phone and wiped her eyes.

Closing the door behind her, Faith placed her hands on her hips. "What's going on, girl?"

Without meeting her sister's gaze, Monica set the phone aside. She stood and began to redress in her street clothes. "I'm not in the mood to try on dresses," she said in a defeated tone. Turning away from Faith, she pulled her top over her head.

Faith gasped at a blue-black mark on Monica's forearm. "My goodness, Monica. How did this happen?" she asked, taking hold of the bruise and glaring at her sister.

Monica snatched her arm away from Faith and continued to dress. She stepped back. "It's—it's nothing. I took a fall in the cafeteria at school, playing around with some of my friends." She laughed nervously. "I slid on something on the floor and fell on my behind. I didn't notice I was bruised until the next day." She shrugged. Then she stood before the mirror. She eyed herself, and then her face crumpled with emotion and she began to cry.

Faith went to Monica and held her. The first thought that crossed her mind was that Ahmad was abusing her little sister.

"You can talk to me. Ahmad did this to you, didn't he?" Faith asked, feeling the rage brew within her.

Monica's dewy eyes met Faith's with fear. "He—he didn't mean to hurt me. It was all my fault. I got angry with him because he was flirting with some girls who were in his face and treating him like he was some NBA superstar. I embarrassed him by interrupting him and making sure the other girls know he was my boyfriend and . . ."

"And what?" Faith demanded.

Monica lowered her chin and tears spilled from her eyes. She remained silent.

"Talk to me."

Wiping her eyes, Monica continued. "He hustled me away and off into the stairwell. He gripped my arm and shoved me against the wall. I'd never seen him so angry. He told me not to ever treat him like that again. He told me no one ran him," she said breathlessly.

"And you're still trying to be with this guy?" Faith asked contemptuously.

"He loves me and I love him. He apologized and even gave me this bracelet to make up for the way he had overreacted." She held up her arm and showed her sister a thin gold bracelet with two lettered charms—*A* and *M*—dangling from it.

Faith urged Monica to sit down and took a seat beside her. "You can't continue seeing Ahmad. He hurt you once, and he'll hurt you again."

"No, he won't. He promised," she said as though she was convinced he wouldn't.

"This isn't love, Monica. Dad and Paula don't want this for you, and neither do I."

Fear sprang into Monica's eyes. "Don't tell them about this. Let me handle this. Everything is going to be fine."

"I can't promise you that, Monica. I'm calling Dad and telling him about Ahmad. If you got hurt any worse, I wouldn't be able to live with myself." Her misery over what Monica was caught up in caused a dull ache in her heart.

Suddenly Monica pulled away from her sister, and her eyes flashed with fury. "I wish you would just keep your mouth shut. You have no right to ruin what I have with Ahmad. Mom and Dad told me about the surprise Gerard sprang on you. Take care of all your baby mama drama and stay out of my business," she lashed out while she finished dressing. Then she stormed out of the dressing room.

Faith went after her into the store, but Monica ran into the mall and got out of sight quickly. Faith's nerves caused her heart to race and her stomach to feel queasy. Immediately she got on the phone and called her father to alert him of what had happened to Monica. She was sure that he would take care of Ahmad and make sure Monica wouldn't see him again.

For the rest of the day, Faith was distracted and troubled over Monica's relationship. She didn't get any relief until her father called her and told her Monica had arrived home and that he and Paula were going to have a serious talk with her and keep a watchful eye on her. Knowing how concerned Faith was, Rufus told her not to worry and to call later. She assured him she would.

It was five thirty when Faith showed up for her shift at the colorful booth that the foundation had prepared. The mall was flooded with people strolling and shopping or just spending a leisurely day browsing and spending time with family or friends.

Reaching the booth, the thought crossed Faith's mind of how she had been working to assist battered and abused women, yet her own sister was in a relationship that could escalate into something awful. She knew she couldn't let that happen.

Greeting her friends Sydney and Nicole, who were helping interested customers, Faith smiled to hide her latest stress. Monica was safe now, she told herself. Her family would help her. It was time for Faith to devote her efforts to the Morning Has Broken Foundation.

Once there was a break in customers, Faith said to Nicole, "I'm glad to see the T-shirts with the butterflies and flowers are really selling well. Not only do the ladies love the bright colors, but they like the fact that we have plenty of sizes for full-figured women."

"We have you to thank for that. After all, you came up with the attractive design," Nicole said. "You know, a lot of women have been taking the pamphlets we have available about the services offered by the foundation. Most have said they know someone or have a relative whom they would like to get involved with what we have to offer."

"I've got a feeling that some of the women who have approached us are asking questions for themselves," Sydney confessed. "As a nurse, I've seen it all, and I can tell by that helpless or defeated look in a person's eyes what's going on." Sydney sighed. "But that's one of the reasons why we're here. Oh, and the mugs we have are right behind the T-shirts in sales. And I don't know if we're going to have enough of the key rings to last for those who are making donations. Folks are really being generous to us."

"There's nothing like one sister reaching out to help another," Faith said. Her eyes were lit up with their success. "I'm so glad we decided to try this. I've been so successful, we've got to make this an annual event. We can use all the funding we can get." Monica flashed in her mind. She grew pensive. Then she said, "It's important to educate women and even teen girls who are caught up in bad relationships. They should know they have options and they don't have to stay."

For the next hour, in between their remaining customers, Faith and her friends were busy discussing the benefits of their foundations or selling merchandise and taking donations. It felt good to Faith to have her mind occupied with other things besides her chaotic personal life.

CHAPTER SEVEN

The next morning, Faith decided to attend the 8:00 A.M. service at Friendship Baptist Church. After the day she'd had, with the stress of Monica's situation and the thrill of raising a huge sum of money for the foundation, she felt church was the place for her to renew her spirits and give thanks.

Seeing his wife making preparations for church, Gerard wanted to go as well. Since she claimed she had no time for him during the week, he knew she wouldn't argue against them attending church together.

Since they didn't arrive promptly at eight, Faith and Gerard slipped quietly into the church and sat in the back pew. During the sermon, Faith caught a glimpse of her father, who sat up front with her stepmother. Normally Rufus worshipped alone, since Paula worked on Sunday mornings. Settling back with Gerard beside her, his arm resting comfortingly around her shoulder, Faith prayed quietly for strength for the changes that were occurring much too fast in her life.

After the benediction, Faith and Gerard exited the church into the cloudy autumn day and walked to the parking area where she knew her father always parked his Town Car.

"Baby, I'll be back in a minute. I see a couple of guys I haven't seen in a while," Gerard said, leaving Faith to wait to speak to her father.

Standing near the car, she broke into a smile when she spotted her father striding toward her, beaming. He embraced her. "I'm glad to see you and Gerard here today. Is this a sign that you're working through the shock of his son coming into your lives?"

Ending their embrace, Faith met her father's gaze. "He's coming whether I like it or not."

"What kind of answer is that?" Her father's brown face was shadowed with concern.

"It's the only thing I have to say about the subject right now."

"Gerard is your husband," he said sternly. "If you love him, you're going to have to support him with what he has to do for his son. And now that you're going to be a mother yourself, you should be even more understanding of what it means to be a parent." Rufus scanned the crowd outside of the church. "What happened to Gerard?"

Gerard appeared as if on cue.

"Dad, how's it going?" He smiled warmly at his father-in-law.

"Fine. Just fine, son. I was telling my daughter how glad I am you two made it today. I hope this becomes more regular now that you're going to become parents."

Suddenly Paula joined them. Dressed in a tailored gray suit, with her brown hair cut in a stylish bob, she looked as though she could have been Faith's big sister. "Good morning. Your father and I were just saying how we hoped you'd find the time to come to church. I can imagine how it's been for both of you, especially now that there's a baby on the way along with Gerard's son to care for."

Looking ill at ease with the mention of Gerard's son, Faith ignored Paula's comment and said, "I didn't expect to see you this morning, Paula. Took a day off from work, huh?"

A flash of annoyance at Faith's lack of acknowledgment to her comment crossed Paula's face. She took hold of Rufus's hand and said, "Yes, hon. I switched my shift for a couple of months. I wanted to spend time with my husband on Sundays. He claimed he was lonely without me." She gave him a smile. "Plus it's been too long since he and I have worshipped together. I'm a staunch believer in 'a family that prays together, stays together.'" She gazed up at Rufus, revealing the warm affection she had for him after nearly nineteen years of marriage. Then she returned her attention to Faith. "Your father and I haven't eaten yet. We left that sister of yours home with orders to begin preparing brunch for us. She still has an attitude over your phone call and the way we've placed restrictions on her and that relationship with Ahmad." She looked worried, then shook it off. "How about you and Gerard joining us? We'd love to have you, and it would give us a chance to discuss family things in private."

"Sounds great to me," Gerard said.

Faith smiled in agreement.

Paula stared at Faith. "How have you been feeling, Faith? I know the first trimester of pregnancy can be difficult for a first-time mom."

"I'm okay. I grow tired quicker than usual, but basically I'm fine."

Rufus looked pleased with his daughter's response as he opened the car door and slid inside. "Well, let's head to the house and deal with the petulant one."

After Faith and her family enjoyed a hearty breakfast of French toast with bacon, coffee, juice and fruit, everyone sat around the table, conversing about things that had occurred during the week.

Monica, who had been made to join them, sat with a somber expression and refused to make eye contact with Faith.

Rufus spoke to Monica. "I should have made you come to church this morning, young lady. The Word could have helped to sweeten your attitude and make you understand how much your family cares for your well-being."

A vague look of despair spread over Monica face. Then she asked, "May I be excused?"

"I want you to clear the table and do these dishes," Paula said in a no-nonsense tone.

Monica sighed in exasperation, jumped to her feet and began hurriedly taking the dishes away.

"What's with her?" Gerard asked, looking puzzled.

"Faith hasn't told you about Monica and what the boy did to her?" Paula asked, giving Faith a baffled look.

"I'm afraid that Faith and I haven't spoken about very much lately—what with our busy schedules and all," Gerard excused himself. "Last night she arrived home worn-out from Fabulous and the foundation work she'd done, and tumbled into bed and fell sound asleep." He chuckled nervously.

Rufus lowered his voice so that Monica couldn't hear him from the kitchen. "Faith called to let me know she had seen bruises on Monica's arm placed there by that Ahmad—that ungrateful . . ." Rufus growled, letting his sentence fade. "I knew he came from a troubled background, but I thought I was getting him on track," he continued in a normal tone. "I didn't like the idea of him taking an interest in Monica. Then I felt like a hypocrite. I didn't want anyone to think my daughter was too good for him. I never imagine she and he would do anything more than casual dating. But then I noticed how cozy and better he seemed to be acting with her in his life. You can't imagine how disappointed I was to learn he had been rough with her."

Paula took her husband's hand. "We've taken care of things. Hopefully Ahmad won't be able to have any contact with Monica again."

Looking disturbed, Gerard leaned forward with interest. "What did you do, Rufus?"

"I went to his house and spoke to him face-to-face. I let him know I wasn't going to tolerate him manhandling my daughter. I also told him I couldn't coach him anymore." Rufus's brow wrinkled. "He wants that professional future, but he'll have to do it without my assistance. He may transfer to another school."

"Good for you, man," Gerard said. "I can imagine Monica isn't going to be pleased with you for awhile."

"She'll get over it. She may not get the reason why at this point, but she will later on," Paula said with determination, stroking Rufus's arm to show her support.

Watching Rufus and Paula, Faith was suddenly hit with memories of her mother and the way Rufus loved her and cared for her. Since she had become pregnant, she'd thought of her mother more. She yearned to share her experiences with Clarice and have her see her through her problems. Faith wondered if her father still thought of her mother. Did he remember what a good and loving woman she'd been?

Clarice Parker had married Faith's father during their freshman year in college. She'd gotten pregnant with Faith soon after, dropped out of school and never returned to get her degree, Faith had learned. Faith remembered her mother being content as a homemaker. At that time, Rufus wasn't able to give her mother the kind of material things he now shared with Paula. Still, Clarice had adored him, and believed there was no one else better than Rufus. His love for her was like a treasure, Clarice had told her young daughter. She'd tell Faith, "Make sure to marry a man as good as your father, and your life will be rich with happiness."

Listening to her father, Gerard and Paula discuss troubled kids and how today's teens were growing up too fast, Faith's mind drifted off to her mother's last days in a hospice. As a heartbroken little girl, Faith stood near her mother, who had grown tiny, thin and pale from the disease that ravished her. Faith was scared and forever haunted by the image. She remembered her mother coming out of one her medicated stupors and smiling wanly at her. She insisted Faith come and sit beside her.

"I can see you're afraid, baby girl. But I don't want you to be sad for me. I'm in God's hands, and that's a good place to be." Clarice spoke with an effort that seemed to make her tired with each word. She managed to smile and hold on tightly to Faith's hand. "Remember the good times you and I shared. Never forget I love you. There's no doubt in my mind you're going to grow into a lovely and smart woman who will make me proud." Then Clarice beckoned her daughter to lean toward her so she could embrace Faith and kiss her once more.

Tears had spilled from her mother's eyes, and Faith's tears had fallen to mingle with her mother's as she held on to her, sobbing and sensing the end. Her father had removed a distraught Faith and eased her into a nearby chair. Then Rufus took his place with his wife. He had kissed her gently and caressed the side of her face lovingly. For a moment, Clarice's eyes had sparkled with love for him. Faith heard her mother say, "Thanks for loving me and taking care of me. Look after our girl. I love you." Then she had exhaled deeply and closed her eyes as though she had drifted into sleep. But Faith knew she was gone by the way her father sobbed shamelessly, holding on to her hand. Faith shook herself as if to shake off the sadness that seemed at times like only yesterday.

As a preteen, Faith had assumed her father would live his life as a single man. She had never expected him to marry again. Who in the world could measure up to her mother? she thought. She felt betrayed when Rufus began to date the twenty-six-year-old Paula. All at once, he had no time for his daughter because he always had plans with Paula. Faith's jealously edged on spite for the woman who had put the twinkle back in her father's eyes. When weekends rolled around, her father relaxed by getting dressed up and splashing on expensive cologne for his dates with the fine nurse she overheard him refer to as his love interest.

Before she knew it, Faith was attending their small wedding ceremony. Though Paula had gone out of her way to be friendly and caring, Faith refused to let Paula get close. She was still loyal to her mother, even if her father was not. Then when Paula became pregnant, Faith had truly felt as though she were an orphan. Although it was Paula's first baby, her father acted as if it were his first as well. When Monica was born, Faith took one look at her sister and fell in love with the fat, cherubic, curly-haired infant. She thought of Monica as half having her father's blood, so that allowed Faith to love the baby in spite of her jealous feelings about Paula's place in Rufus's life. She continued to keep Paula at arm's length. She'd had a mother to love her and didn't want to share that special kind of love with another woman.

Faith's reverie was broken when she felt Gerard's arm around her shoulder and realized everyone was looking at her.

"Elijah will be with us very soon," Gerard was saying.

Paula leaned on the table and stared at Faith as though she were trying to read her mind. "What a turn your lives have taken. You've just gotten married, and now there are going to be two children. I'm sure you will deal well with this." She gave Faith a sympathetic look. "You can count on your father and me to help as much as we can."

"The games women play," Rufus mumbled. "How dare this Iris keep your son from you all these years?" he said to Gerard.

"I can't believe what's going on myself," Gerard replied. "Iris said she didn't want anything to do with me and didn't think the child would want to either. She made sure I wasn't that important. Now she wants to ditch the kid on me and go off and pretend she's single. Iris isn't doing this for Elijah's benefit. She wants to be free to do what she wants."

"What a shame to desert her child," Paula said. "Poor boy."

Faith remained silent. She didn't want to say anything she might regret in front of Rufus and Paula.

Gerard stared at his wife and squeezed her arm. "This isn't anything I wanted to put Faith through. Yet, since I have the proof I'm Elijah's father, I can't turn my back on him."

Disentangling herself, Faith got up and left for the kitchen. She was glad that there was no sign of Monica, although she was ready for the confrontation she knew was coming. Unexpectedly, Rufus followed Faith into the kitchen.

Faith went to the fridge for a bottle of water. She unscrewed the top, took a long drink and turned to face a concerned Rufus, who stood nearby. She sighed heavily before she spoke.

"I wanted to be the first one to give him children," she said aloud for the first time. "I never dreamed I'd have to share Gerard with someone else the way I had to learn to share you after Mom died." The moment the words slipped from her mouth, she regretted them. Paula had come silently into the kitchen, and out of the corner of her eye Faith saw her flinch. "I'm sorry. I didn't mean it like it sounded."

Paula gave her a lenient nod. "You and I had our issues when I came into your father's life. I knew you resented me, but I also knew you were too young to understand how much your father and I loved each other. I never tried to take your mother's place in your life. Now you're in the position I was in. It works out, Faith. I love your father, and I came to love you like you were my own because you were his and because you were so caring and loving of Monica. We took it one day at a time, one problem at a time. That's all you can do." She softened her voice. "Marriage is beautiful. You savor all the joy and happiness you share so much that, when the bad times or the challenges come, you have something to strive for to put everything back into perspective."

"Paula is right," Rufus agreed. "We're here for you. You're going to need all the support you can get in your condition. I don't want you to become stressed. I want a healthy and happy grandchild. Let's go back in the living room, where your husband is waiting for you." He looked kindly at his daughter. "He's a good guy. He feels terrible about all of this. He needs you, Faith. He needs us too."

Faith nodded. "You guys go on. Give me a minute to collect myself."

Rufus and Paula left her.

Sipping her bottled water, Faith was glad she'd been straightforward with her father and Paula about the whirlwind of changes in her life. However, she wasn't sure if she was capable of dealing with the inevitable issue. What in the world was she to do with the eight-year-old stranger who was coming into her home? She had this foreboding that Elijah wasn't going to be there for a short visit like Iris claimed.

Trying to stop her thoughts of Elijah, Faith thought of Monica. Faith set aside her bottle of water and headed for her sister's room. There she found Monica stretched out on her bed wearing the earplugs from her iPod. Monica's eyes were closed as she sang the sad lyrics off-key. Faith dropped down on the bed beside her. Monica jumped and bolted upright. "You scared me to death," she snapped. "What do you want?" Frowning, she snatched out the earplugs.

"I came to talk to you. I want you to know I called Daddy because I care, girl. What kind of sister would I be if I kept quiet about what I'd seen?"

Faith argued. "You can't continue with Ahmad and think you're in some fantastic relationship."

"I told it would never happen again. Why couldn't you have believed me?"

Faith held up her hand to cut Monica off. "Now we're sure it won't. I have met women who have been abused. I've heard them tell how they lied to friends and relatives about clumsy falls and walking into doors when all along it was their husband or boyfriend who was battering them."

Monica gnawed her lip thoughtfully, and she looked caught. "Ahmad and I had a problem. It wasn't something that wasn't fixable between us until you opened your mouth and ruined everything." She fell back onto her bed and turned away from Faith. "Daddy is trying to get Ahmad transferred, and he has made it clear that Ahmad and I aren't to see each other anymore." Her voice quavered. "I suppose I have you to thank for embarrassing me and ruining the good thing I had with Ahmad."

"I'm sorry you feel that way. But I'm with Dad and Paula on this one." She got up to leave and heard her sister crying. Faith knew she and her family were going to have to keep a watchful eye on Monica. They weren't dealing with a little girl anymore, but instead a developing young woman who needed guidance. Most important, she needed to be kept away from guys like Ahmad who could only ruin her life.

CHAPTER EIGHT

It was a little past one o'clock in the afternoon, and Faith had been in her store office, dealing with paperwork and placing orders for new stock, when she glanced at the security camera and saw Gerard chatting with Tasha.

"Hi there," he said when he finally made his way to her small office. He came to her side and kissed her, then he took a seat on the corner of her desk.

"What are you doing away from the bank this time of day?" Faith asked, leaning on her elbows.

"I had to rent my tux for the ball." He rubbed his hands together and said, "And . . . I went to my attorney's office."

Faith felt her heart quiver with anxious anticipation. "What business did you have to take care of with him?"

"I wanted to have papers drawn up so that I can

make sure I'll have joint custody of Elijah. I wanted them to be ready when Iris brings him to us."

Falling back in her seat, Faith closed her eyes and felt angry tears begin to well.

"Don't look that way, baby. I want my rights with Elijah. It's going to be an adjustment, but we can work through this."

She didn't want to accept this reality, especially since he had never consulted her about custody. "I wish I could feel as optimistic as you."

Gerard stood and went to stand behind her. He placed his hands on her shoulders. "Give Elijah a chance. That's all I ask." He kissed the top of her head.

Leaning away from him, Faith gave him a dubious look. "Have you spoken to Iris about this custody matter?"

He strolled to the front of her desk and loosened his tie. "Yes, I have. She was all right with the legal arrangements for custody." He stared at her.

Faith's stomach contracted into a tight ball. "I'm sure she's all set to deliver him."

"She'll be bringing him Saturday evening," he informed her. "We have to get busy and prepare for him."

Lowering her eyes, Faith began to fumble through some papers on her desk.

"When can you go shopping with me, so we can get what we need in his room?"

Wincing, Faith said, "I really have a lot to do in the next few days. Why don't you get Alex to help

GET UP TO
4 FREE BOOKS!

You can have the best romance delivered to your door for less than what you'd pay in a bookstore or online. Sign up for one of our book clubs today, and we'll send you **FREE* BOOKS** just for trying it out...with no obligation to buy, ever!

HISTORICAL ROMANCE BOOK CLUB

Travel from the Scottish Highlands to the American West, the decadent ballrooms of Regency England to Viking ships. Your shipments will include authors such as CONNIE MASON, SANDRA HILL, CASSIE EDWARDS, JENNIFER ASHLEY, LEIGH GREENWOOD, and many, many more.

LOVE SPELL BOOK CLUB

Bring a little magic into your life with the romances of Love Spell—fun contemporaries, paranormals, time-travels, futuristics, and more. Your shipments will include authors such as LYNSAY SANDS, CJ BARRY, COLLEEN THOMPSON, NINA BANGS, MARJORIE LIU and more.

As a book club member you also receive the following special benefits:

- **30% OFF** all orders through our website & telecenter!
- **Exclusive access to** special discounts!
- **Convenient** home delivery **and 10 day examination period to return any books you don't want to keep.**

There is no minimum number of books to buy, and you may cancel membership at any time. See back to sign up!

*Please include $2.00 for shipping and handling.

YES!

Sign me up for the **Historical Romance Book Club** and send my TWO FREE BOOKS! If I choose to stay in the club, I will pay only $8.50* each month, a savings of $5.48!

YES!

Sign me up for the **Love Spell Book Club** and send my TWO FREE BOOKS! If I choose to stay in the club, I will pay only $8.50* each month, a savings of $5.48!

NAME: _____

ADDRESS: _____

_____

TELEPHONE: _____

E-MAIL: _____

☐ **I WANT TO PAY BY CREDIT CARD.**

☐ VISA   ☐ MasterCard   ☐ DISCOVER

ACCOUNT #: _____

EXPIRATION DATE: _____

SIGNATURE: _____

Send this card along with $2.00 shipping & handling for each club you wish to join, to:

**Romance Book Clubs
20 Academy Street
Norwalk, CT 06850-4032**

Or fax (must include credit card information!) to: 610.995.9274.
You can also sign up online at www.dorchesterpub.com.

*Plus $2.00 for shipping. Offer open to residents of the U.S. and Canada only.
Canadian residents please call 1.800.481.9191 for pricing information.
If under 18, a parent or guardian must sign. Terms, prices and conditions subject to change. Subscription subject
to acceptance. Dorchester Publishing reserves the right to reject any order or cancel any subscription.

you? I'm clueless as to what a little boy would want."

Irked by her cool, aloof manner, Gerard stood straighter. "No problem, I'll take care of things. It looks as though you're going to need more time to get used to all this."

Faith ignored his irritation. "Did I mention we're having Thanksgiving dinner with my folks?"

He ran his hand over his face. "Wow! That's next week. Hey, that's fine with me. Elijah will be here. This will give him a chance to get to know your side of the family."

Gerard leaned over and kissed Faith again. He placed a hand under her chin to level her gaze with his. "It's going to be okay. Just remember I love you, and what we have on the way too." He gave her a dazzling smile that lit up his handsome face. "I've got to get back to work. I wanted to tell you the news face-to-face. See you at home later."

"Uh, yeah, see you later," Faith said, knowing she couldn't hide her feelings of frustration.

When Gerard left her office, she glanced at the security camera, watching him swagger out of Fabulous with one hand in his slacks pocket. He passed two women who sized him up with admiring glances. Gerard smiled at the women and spoke cheerfully, leaving them giggling as he left the store. Though he had tried not to appear eager, Faith could see that Elijah's visit and the fact that Gerard was going to make him a part of their life was important to him.

Tasha came into the office shortly after Gerard left.

"It's not too busy. Casey can handle the floor traffic. I'm going to have a cup of coffee and a bit of conversation with you." She gave Faith a questioning look and poured water into her mug over some instant coffee. "Your husband is in a good mood today. Has he gotten a promotion or something?"

"I wish," Faith said in a tone of resignation. "*His* son will be arriving soon, and he's arranging for custody of him."

Tasha stared at her. "Obviously you're not that excited about being a stepmom."

"Not really, but there's nothing I can do." Faith briefly explained in depth the situation she had only glazed over with Tasha until now. "He'll be arriving this weekend and has to stay at least until after the first of the year."

Tasha gave Faith a sympathetic look. "Oh, my goodness. You are going to have your hands full, aren't you?"

"If only all of this could have happened after I had my baby," Faith confessed "I wanted to be the only woman to have Gerard's children. It would have been so meaningful to share being a parent for the first time with Gerard. But I feel my pregnancy won't be as big a deal, with Elijah coming into his life. He has a child—a son. I always dreamed of having a family with the same father and mother. I know it may appear selfish on my part, but it's what I wanted. I want to share my life—our baby's life—with Gerard only. My dreams held no room for an intruder. I'd never imagined I would be involved in the midst of a baby mama drama that his ex has given me."

"Don't linger on all of this," Tasha said softly. "You're only upsetting yourself. Gerard loves you, and I know how you love him. This will work. You're a strong woman, and I know you will have a fine blended family."

"Blended family. What a mess," Faith said slowly. "Elijah's arrival will be out of my control and I have to take it to maintain my marriage." She sighed and gave Tasha a modest smile to hide the negative feelings she harbored; then she changed the subject to the stock that was due to arrive in the next few days in time for the holidays.

"You owe me big time," Alex said as they shopped in JC Penney. "I gave up a date with a sure thing to help you shop for your son."

Gerard grinned at his friend and compared bed linen—a cartoon-themed set as opposed to a sports-themed set. "Elijah is going to love you, man. Yes indeed, he's going to love Mr. Alex for his generosity. I'm counting on you to help me ease Elijah into my life. Right now Faith isn't too thrilled. I haven't given up on her, though. I'm sure once we both get to know Elijah, all this ridiculous tension will disappear." Gerard rubbed his head thoughtfully at the choices of linen. "I don't know what to get for the kid. I don't know his likes or dislikes. Maybe we better go with some plaid stuff like that blue and red stuff over there." He pointed to a corner, where he wandered with Alex following him.

Alex urged Gerard to go with everything plaid, from the bed linens, to the curtains. Then he said, "I can't believe the soap opera you're in the middle of, man. You're the drama king."

"I'm trying to maintain my composure through all this. It's important I make Elijah feel welcomed and wanted. I'm not going to get caught up in the fact that Faith can't stand Iris and that Iris isn't too cool on Faith," Gerard said. He picked up several sets of sheets, two pairs of curtains, and a comforter, and hauled everything to the counter. "Alex, check out that lamp with the football as a base. I'd like that if I was an eight-year-old, but will my boy like it?" he mused. "Shoot, get it, man. If he's not into sports, you and I can work on creating an interest in him."

"Yeah," Alex agreed quickly. "If he's going to hang out with us, he's bound to get the sports fever. Once you and Faith get to know him, maybe you, me and he can get together for a man's meal and a movie—action or karate."

"I'm glad to see you're getting into this with me. I want you to spend time with him, too. After all, you're like a brother to me. I'd like for him to think of you as an uncle he can hang with, especially when we need a baby-sitter."

"Baby-sitter? Me?" Alex said, looking amused. "I'm supposed to be a lover, man."

"Don't worry, it won't tarnish your ladies'-man reputation. In fact, you might get points with your ladies when they find out you're sensitive enough to care for a kid. Just think how you're going to impress Eva Carey. Did you get around to asking her to that charity ball yet?"

Alex's hazel eyes flashed with mischief. "Yeah, I sure did. She told me she'd have to check her schedule. I'm sure she's going with me, though. She just wants to make me sweat a bit." He shook his head.

"What are you going to do if Eva doesn't go with you?" Gerard asked, grinning.

"The ladies love me, man. She's going with me, and I'm going to turn up the charm. She's special."

"Hmm . . . sounds as though you're being pulled into the settling-down mode."

"This woman Eva could make me want this if she lets me get close to her," Alex said thoughtfully. Then his face brightened. "I hope you use her as your pediatrician. I'll be more than willing to take that boy of yours."

"That's good to know. I'm going to need a good nurse and baby-sitter like you." Gerard chuckled.

"Wait until the fellas hear that Alex Washington is a baby-sitter. I'll never hear the end of it, man," Alex said, slapping Gerard on the back. "But your kid is the only one I'm keeping. I won't have the other married guys we know turning me into their nanny." He laughed quietly, watching his friend shell out several large bills for all the stuff they'd selected.

"I heard that," Gerard said. He took a few bags from the clerk and Alex took the others.

"When will the little man be arriving in Bellamy?" Alex asked.

"Saturday evening. Although Faith had no time to shop with me, she agreed to take off from work to help me greet him and get him settled."

Alex grunted. "You'll be in my prayers. You've got a wife who is angry, an ex-wife who is selfish and little boy who is a complete stranger to you. You don't know whether he's going to resent you or grow to love you as his daddy."

Gerard grinned wryly. "I'm going to make it work. I have no other choice. I know it's not going to be easy, but I'm going to pull my family together," he said with conviction.

As he and Alex strolled into the mall, Gerard was consumed with mixed emotions. He was grateful he had been able to get Faith to leave her store early on Saturday to be there for Elijah. He didn't expect her to embrace him completely, yet he hoped she would make Elijah feel wanted. He was more than ready to get to know his son. The moment he had seen the pictures and had seen the resemblance between himself and Elijah, Gerard had made a place in his heart for him. He didn't want to be put in the awkward position of proving whom he loved better—Faith, the baby that was on the way or Elijah.

CHAPTER NINE

The Saturday that Elijah was to arrive in town, Faith regretted agreeing to leave the store early. She had been anxious and distracted for most of the day.

Knowing of Faith's situation, Tasha had tried her best to keep her involved with work-related issues and idle gossip.

When five o'clock rolled around and Faith prepared to leave for home, Tasha met her in the office.

"Relax, boss. Don't look for things to be perfect. It's not going to feel right for a while," Tasha advised. "The main thing is that you're showing your man you're making an effort. I know from my own experiences with my ups and down how that is appreciated."

Faith looked saturnine. "Sure, I'll do that. I have no other choice." She stood and grabbed her purse and her coat. She shrugged. "It'll only be for a few months that I'll have to deal with Elijah on an everyday basis."

Tasha nodded encouragingly. "Exactly. Like I keep telling you, you're a strong woman and you have a good heart. This is going to be a cinch for you."

Suddenly Faith closed her eyes, exhaled loudly and scowled. She dropped back down in her chair. "I'm so angry with Iris for putting this on us at this time. She should have waited another couple of years to focus on her career. She could have found out what we were doing, if we could handle it. She could have given me and Gerard a chance to know each other as husband and wife and to enjoy our child. If she'd done that, I wouldn't feel as used or resentful."

Tasha gave her a sympathetic look. "You've got to let go of your negative feelings. There are children involved. You don't want your stress to cause any complications that could affect your pregnancy."

Rising to her feet with determination, Faith sighed. "You're right. My feelings don't count. Right now it's all about Elijah," she said. "Call me if you run into any problems here." She left the office, with Tasha following her to return to the store to assist customers.

"Don't worry about Fabulous. The girls and I can take care of everything. I'll be thinking about you," Tasha called to Faith. "I'll give you a call when I get home tonight to let you know how things went here and to see how things went at home for you."

"Thanks, Tasha," Faith said, walking slowly out of the store as though she was going to a funeral.

Turning her car onto her street, Faith spotted a shiny black SUV in her driveway. She assumed it had brought Iris and Elijah. Just for a second she considered passing by her house and going for a drive until she believed Iris had left. She realized that was foolish. This was her home, and no one was going to run her out of it.

Faith came through the door and heard Iris speaking loudly. She quietly followed the sounds of the voice to the living room to find Elijah, awkward yet pleased, leaning on Gerard's knee. Gerard whispered something into the boy's ear that made his eyes light up with glee.

"Elijah, come on, smile big for Legend, baby. I want to have a good picture to remember you while you're away from me," Iris urged her son while the camera was held by a big guy dressed in jeans and a brightly colored shirt with platinum chains dangling around his neck. The man had an arrogance about him that clearly said he was some kind of celebrity.

Iris dressed in poured-on jeans with stiletto heels peeking from underneath. She wore a silky camisole baring her shoulders. Her spiky do was replaced with long hair down her back. A weave job, no doubt, Faith mused. Iris looked as though she was set to go out clubbing. She made the trendy Faith feel dowdy in her casual red pantsuit.

"There's that smile I love. It's just like your daddy's." She instructed the guy who Faith assumed was her man to click away, and touched the man on the shoulder to end the session. "Come give me a big hug. I'm going to miss you, little man, but I'll have these pictures to keep near me. Gerard—your daddy—is going to take good care of you while I'm off working." She gave Legend an affectionate wink. "I won't have to worry about you, because you're with your people." She hugged her son to her.

Faith watched the young boy lock his arms around his mother's neck. Then Elijah saw Faith. He released his mother. "Who is she?" he asked.

Gerard, Iris and the big man turned their attention toward Faith, who they hadn't realized had arrived home.

Iris smirked and tossed her hair over her shoulder. "You've sneaked up on us. Again."

Iris's remark grated on Faith's nerves. Faith shot her a penetrating glare.

Sensing trouble, Gerard jumped to his feet and met Faith with a kiss on her cheek. "I'm glad you're here." He took her by the hand and led her to Elijah, who clung shyly to Iris's side. "This is Elijah. Elijah, this is my wife, Faith. She's going to help me look after you."

Elijah gave his mother a wide-eyed look filled with angst. "Will I have to call her 'Mommy'?"

There was an uncomfortable silence.

"No, you won't, dear," Faith responded with a hint of a smile. " 'Faith' will do just fine. You only have one mother." Now that she had seen Elijah in person, there was no denying Gerard was his father. He had the same eyes, skin coloring and endearing smile. The boy was cute.

"Faith, I'd like you to meet my man, Legend. He's a rapper you're going to be hearing a lot about very soon. He's already a big hit on the West Coast." Standing beside the big man, who was the size of a football player, Iris hooked her arm with his and grinned like a teen girl in love. "Legend, this is Gerard's bride, Faith."

The man nodded politely and extended his hand. "Hey. Nice to meet you."

Faith smiled and accepted his hand, noticing the flashy diamond-studded watch on his wrist and the huge diamond rings he wore as well. From the designer jeans and shirt and the expensive jewelry the rapper wore, Faith assumed Iris had landed herself a man with plenty of money to give her the kind of lifestyle she wanted.

Iris thrust the camera at Legend. "Baby, take one more picture for me," she insisted. "C'mon, Gerard," she ordered. "It will be nice for Elijah to have one with his mommy and daddy. I'll have it framed and send it to him."

Faith simmered, watching the way Gerard hopped to Iris's command and got into position on the other side of Elijah.

Studying the three elated family members, Faith felt as though she were a stranger in her own home. Déjà vu, she mused. Hadn't she been there and done that with her father, his new wife and the baby they'd had during the most vulnerable time in her life? Her father had thoughtlessly made Faith take pictures of himself, Paula and Monica when he had brought them home from the hospital.

Faith turned away from them and fought the urge to flee the room. Yet she didn't want to give Iris the satisfaction of knowing she had the ability to get next to her or to make her uncomfortable in the home Faith and Gerard had planned for their life and their own children.

Iris stooped down to Elijah's level and said, "Well, it's time for Mommy to leave. I've packed all of your favorite toys and videos. Your father told me he intends to take you shopping. Don't be shy about telling him what you need or want. Your old man can afford to get you whatever you want." She winked at Gerard.

Elijah leaned on his mother, looking as though he wanted to cry. "How long will you be gone this time, Mom?"

Rolling her eyes impatiently, Iris said, "Come on, little man. You and I have gone over all of this several times. You know I have to work. You know how we'll be traveling all over the country to become big stars. You watch that music show on BET, and you'll see Legend or me in a video. I've explained it all to you. Now it's your daddy's turn to enjoy you and to see what a good little boy you are." She grabbed her short fur coat and slipped it on with Legend's assistance.

Elijah glanced at Gerard, who hovered near him. Then Elijah made an effort at whispering, but his words were heard distinctly. "Do I have to call him 'Dad'? I don't want to, Mom."

Looking embarrassed, Iris gazed down at her son. "You'll get used to it, son. Gerard is your daddy. Try to grow up to be a good man like him. Remember how I explained to you how your father and I have become friends for your sake. He and I will always have your best interests at heart." She glanced at Legend, who pointed at his watch. "I've got to get on the road, baby. I have to go off and make you proud of me."

She smiled nervously at Gerard and Faith. "I'm ready, baby," she said to Legend, who made his way out of the house after mumbling a hasty good-bye.

Fear filled Elijah's eyes. "I don't want you to go and leave me, Mommy. I want to be with you and near my friends," he whined.

"Elijah, be a big boy for Mommy," Iris chided. "I don't have time for you to act ugly. Legend is waiting for me, and we've got to get on the road to meet some important people. I keep telling you the same thing over and over again." She went up to him, held his face, and placed a smacking kiss on his forehead that left a trace of her bright lipstick. "I'll be in touch as often as I can." She stared at him, released him and dashed out the door.

Elijah attempted to go after her, but Gerard caught hold of him and tried to calm him and assure him he would be fine with them. The more Gerard spoke, the more loudly Elijah cried.

Faith couldn't bear the sight of the boy sobbing. It was obvious the child didn't like the idea of being left with strangers. If she wanted Elijah to know Gerard, it appeared she would have come up with an arrangement that would make it easier for Elijah to make the transition. Poor Elijah was being forced into the situation the same way she had been. He was as voiceless as she had been with what life had given them.

With a mumbled excuse, Faith left Gerard alone with Elijah to comfort him, and headed for the kitchen to prepare a cup of tea.

After a while, Gerard appeared in the kitchen, looking emotionally drained. He dropped down on a chair across from where Faith sat scanning a magazine and sipping peppermint tea to ease the nausea she had begun to experience upon her return home. Since she had discovered she was pregnant, she had bouts of morning sickness when she first awoke, but never in the evening. She assumed that Iris's presence and the arrival of Elijah had added to her discomfort. In the past few days, after she learned of Gerard's son's coming, she'd had more frequent bouts of queasiness.

"How did you get your son to quiet down?" Faith asked coolly. She was annoyed that Gerard had come to her as though he was looking for solace. She supposed he expected this, since she had taken off from work because he had asked her.

His eyes drooped with concern. "Television is like a sedative to the kid, Iris told me. I found something for him to watch. Right now, he's confused and sad," Gerard said, jiggling his knee.

"His mother has forced a lot of stuff on him at one time," she said in a judgmental tone. "The poor child. I mean, one minute she tells him he has a father who has been too busy and uninterested in him, and the next minute she's shoving him at this father and trying to convince the kid he's the best thing in the world. The boy is bound to be frustrated and confused—especially seeing his mother going off without a care with that man," she ranted.

Frowning, Gerard sighed heavily. He searched Faith's face for the sympathy he thought he heard in her voice. "I'm worried about that, too. She treats Elijah like a little adult. You should see the designer clothes and all the toys he has. I believe she's one of those parents who comforts her kid with material things, instead of with her time and attention."

"You're coming with us Monday, aren't you?" Gerard's brow creased, and he gave Faith a pleading look. "I'd like to show the school that Elijah has family support. I'd really appreciate you being with us."

She pursed her lips and shook her head. This was something she didn't want to do. Several of the teachers at the school Elijah was to attend were sorors of hers or worked in the Morning Has Broken Foundation. She would be too ashamed. "You don't really need me. I simply can't make it," she said as an excuse. "I'm going to be extremely busy in the next few months. Not only do I have to restock the store, but I have to help Tasha supervise the extra help we've hired for the holidays. And with our baby coming, I'm going to have to pace myself to make sure *our* child is healthy," she reminded him.

Gerard's eyes grew dark with disappointment. Stress lines formed on his brow. "We're parents, Faith," he said in a controlled tone. "I care about our baby too. So why can't you share an interest in Elijah?"

"You sure haven't shown much interest in me or my condition," Faith said, feeling the heat rise in her face. "You ran out and bought new things for Elijah's room, but you weren't thoughtful enough to take the time to even buy a teddy bear or a rattle for this child," she said, not able to hide her annoyance.

Gerard looked ashamed. "I'm sorry, sweetheart, but I do care. It's just with all this stuff involving

Elijah, I felt it was more immediate. I wanted to make sure I made him feel welcomed and comfortable in his new surroundings. Besides, we have months to get what we need for the baby." He moved closer to her. "Forgive me if I haven't taken the proper time to speak with you about your condition. You look lovely and radiant, so I'm guessing things must be great for you." He reached over to take her hand; then he scooted beside her and placed his palm on her tummy. "How is *our* baby?"

His touch and his eyes, warm with delight, reminded Faith of the love she still harbored for him. "So far, so good. I'm sick in the morning and I get tired quickly," Faith admitted. She beamed at him, wishing there could only be him, her and the impending birth of their child to absorb the love of their new marriage.

"Baby's under construction," he said, chuckling. He lavished her with a tender smile.

Just as they had made intimate eye contact and Faith had grown cozy with her loving emotions, Elijah burst through the door and stood in the middle of the floor. She was dismayed by the way Gerard jumped away from her as though he had been caught doing something wrong.

"I want a drink," Elijah demanded, looking glum. He stood wringing his hands.

Gerard bolted to his feet and went to the fridge, then paused. " 'May I have a drink,' " Gerard reprimanded the boy.

Elijah glanced at Faith, who had interlocked her hands over her tummy and was offering him a hint of a smile.

Elijah hesitated before saying, "May I have a drink?"

"That's better," Gerard said. "What kind of drink, son?" He pulled open the refrigerator door. "We have juice, milk and soda."

Elijah ambled to the fridge and snatched a can of orange soda.

"Let me open it for you," Gerard offered.

"I can do it," Elijah insisted, fumbling with the tab until he opened the drink, causing it to spray right in Faith's face and on her red outfit.

As Faith let out a yelp from the unexpected spray of soda and jumped to her feet, Elijah giggled with glee. The can tilted in his hand and spilled more soda onto the floor.

"Elijah, that's not funny. You apologize for what you did," Gerard ordered. He reached for paper towels and went to his wife to wipe her face. "Elijah, I can't hear you," he said sternly.

Faith caught a glimpse of Elijah looking chagrined, with tears welling in his eyes. He didn't say anything. He turned and ran out of the room.

As Gerard wiped the soda from her face and dabbed at her clothes, Faith took the towels from him. "I'll take care of this myself." She said. "Go check on him. No telling what he might be tearing up now that he knows he's angered you."

"Give the kid a chance, Faith. He made a mistake, and I can see he needs to learn some manners, but he's not a monster. He needs some structure that we can give him."

Holding up her hand, Faith said, "I'm not in the mood to go into all of this at the moment. You keep an eye on him." She stormed from the kitchen, wondering how she was going to be able to live with Elijah over the next few months.

While she was changing out of her stained clothes, Gerard entered the bedroom. "It was a harmless mishap," he said. "He didn't mean it. Give him a chance to apologize. All of us are a bit nervous being alone together for the first time."

Examining the spotty places on her suit, Faith mindlessly said, "Yeah, I bet he does. He probably got a kick out of what he did. I bet his mother has probably talked about me to him as though I'm not to be taken seriously."

"I doubt that," Gerard said. "Don't make it more than the accident that it was." His voice was soft. Gerard slipped behind her and kissed the back of her neck. "Please be patient. We need time to get used to being around one another."

Faith shrugged away from Gerard and tossed her clothes onto a nearby chair. She lay down on the bed and turned away from her husband. "I'm tired. There's been too much tension for me. I'm going to take a nap to relax."

"That's a good idea. I'll be in the other room watching television. When you awake, I want us to go out for dinner to celebrate Elijah's arrival. I have a special gift to give him so he'll remember this day."

Faith rolled on her back and stared at Gerard. "I feel a headache coming on. I'm not in the mood to eat out. Just leave me alone." She turned away from him. "Why don't you order a pizza or something? I'm sure that's what he's used to anyway."

Gerard flinched. "It may be, but I want us to go out together. The sooner we start treating him as a member of the Wynn family, the more comfortable he'll feel. Faith, can't you do this for me?" His voice carried an edge of indignation.

Faith wouldn't look at him. She couldn't. Tears of frustration were spilling down her eyes. "I'm not up for this, Gerard," she said curtly. "Go on without me."

"I can't believe how stubborn you're being," he said hotly. "You're not sick. You're only having a baby. It's not fair to take your bitterness out on Elijah." He left the room, closing the door behind him harder than he normally did.

Now that she was alone, Faith's feelings switched from frustration to jealousy. Gerard hadn't done anything yet to celebrate the news of their new child. Caught up in the swirl of drama, he hadn't even been considerate enough to give her flowers or a thoughtful present the way he used to express his feelings for her before he knew of Elijah. It was as if Gerard had forgotten how much this baby meant to her. The significance of their parenthood had lost its importance since Iris had appeared and taken away Faith's privilege of making him a father for the first time. Exhausted from her thoughts, Faith fell asleep and didn't awaken until a couple of hours later.

Once she was out of bed, she left the bedroom and found the house silent. She assumed Gerard had taken the boy out for their special evening. She ventured into the bedroom Gerard had prepared for Elijah. She deliberately avoided the room and had no idea what he and Alex had done with it. One day curiosity got the best of her and she peeked inside the boy's room. Faith couldn't help but admire the room with the red-and-blue plaid linens and matching curtains. Gerard had spared no expense. Elijah's closet had been filled jackets, coats and sports gear that his father had bought. Then there was a television with its own DVD player and a Playstation 2. He had a mini-basketball hoop along with a spongy basketball. Faith was sure Gerard was going to get Elijah involved in recreational sports with the other kids in the neighborhood. He was going to be one of those fathers who was going to attempt to groom a prize athlete, she assumed.

Tonight, making her second visit to the room, she saw the clutter of suitcases and boxes of toys Elijah had brought from the home he had shared with Iris. Gerard had just flung things on the boy's bed, and here and there about the floor. He and Elijah should have straightened the room before they went gallivanting off to their celebration. Faith glanced at her watch and noticed it was nearly eight o'clock. Gerard was going to have a lot to do to his room before Elijah could get into bed.

Turning to leave the room, Faith's foot slipped on a toy truck on the floor. Her leg flew out from under her, causing her to lose her balance and hit the floor hard, landing so hard on her bottom that it made her stomach convulse with pain. Yowling, she doubled over in agony. As she made an effort to stand, she felt moistness between her legs. Panic-stricken, she broke out in a cold sweat, fearing for her baby.

Stark fear crawled through her as she stumbled to the bathroom to check herself. When she saw her bloodstained panties, she shuddered and let out a moan of despair. She staggered from the bathroom and to her bedroom to call her obstetrician's answering service. Frantically, she explained her condition to the operator. While she waited for the doctor's return call, she lay on her bed, fearing the worst. Was this the price for being selfish?

Gerard arrived home with Elijah in tow. The phone rang, and both he and Faith answered. Hearing Dr. Wells identify herself to Faith, he held on and listened to his wife's strained voice explain her mishap. Learning that the doctor wanted Faith to get to the emergency room, Gerard hung up the phone and rushed into the bedroom, where he discovered Faith in tears, clutching her middle.

"What happened, baby?" Gerard asked.

Elijah followed his father into their bedroom and stood watching Faith, who was crying in Gerard's arms.

Gerard helped a pain-racked and fearful Faith off of the bed. "Let's get you to the hospital. Things might not be as bad as they seem," he encouraged her, trying not to worry himself. He spotted his son watching them. "Elijah, go and get our coats. We have to take Faith to the hospital," he explained in a calm tone.

The boy dashed away on his mission.

"Gerard, I want this baby. I can't lose it," Faith cried in desperation. "I love it. I want to be a mother."

Gerard tightened his arms around her waist. "You will. It's going to be all right," he said in a confident tone, not only to boost her, but to convince himself. He knew all this business over the discovery of his son and Elijah's arrival into their lives had stressed Faith. He didn't want to be responsible for her miscarrying. If that happened, he knew Faith would be thrown into a terrible emotional state and would hold it against him—and, worse still, against Elijah.

CHAPTER TEN

Faith wasn't in the mood to celebrate Thanksgiving. Her father and Paula insisted that she come to dinner with Gerard and Elijah. It had been a week since Faith had lost her baby. Dr. Wells assured them that her tripping over the toy hadn't caused the miscarriage. In fact, the doctor told Faith she would be able to try for another baby in three months, and that the next pregnancy would probably be more successful.

Faith didn't feel any consolation. People who made love had babies, and she surely didn't feel the same kind of passion toward Gerard in order to conceive again. Why would he want another child now? He had a healthy son he hardly knew how to deal with.

Faith felt empty, depressed and like a failure because she had lost the child they'd conceived during the most beautiful time of her life, their honeymoon. Nothing could replace that moment, the kind of joy she felt knowing she was going to be a mother despite her insecurities over Elijah.

Released from the hospital within twenty-four hours of losing her baby, Faith returned home not wanting to share her feelings of loss. Instead she took to her bed and forced herself to sleep to shut Gerard out. Today was her first day out of the house.

With Monica's assistance, Paula had prepared a lovely turkey dinner. Faith put on her game face and pretended all was well. She joined conversations and complimented the meal. After dinner, Gerard and Rufus took Elijah outside to toss around a football to burn calories.

Faith went to the kitchen with Monica and Paula and attempted to help with the dishes, but she was ordered to take a seat and to keep them company with conversation.

Faith didn't have much to say. She knew that Monica was only being nice to her because of the miscarriage. She could still sense that her sister was peeved with her for ruining what everyone but Monica considered a dysfunctional relationship. So their conversation was reduced to their Christmas wishes and the shopping and chores that had to be done for the holidays.

"Faith, don't worry about getting a baby-sitter for that charity ball. You can count on your father and me to look after Elijah. He can spend the night with us, so you and Gerard can have a wonderful evening," Paula said. "I'm sure getting all dolled up for that fabulous event will be uplifting to both of you."

"Thanks, I'm sure Gerard will appreciate that," Faith said, unable to build any enthusiasm for the ball at the moment.

Then Faith moved out of her seat and went to the kitchen window, where she saw Gerard tossing the football to Elijah, who caught it and held it proudly. Rufus urged Elijah to throw to him then he tossed it back his way. Once again, Elijah made a good catch. Faith saw Gerard pump his arm with pride. His action placed a broad grin on Elijah's face.

Faith was reminded of the dream she'd had on her honeymoon of Gerard and their son playing Frisbee. Could she have had a premonition of Elijah's arrival?

"Faith, dear, will you slice the sweet potato pie for me? Those men are going to be looking for dessert when they come in." Paula set the plates before her on the counter. "I'm glad you came out today." She smiled at Faith.

"So am I," Faith said.

"How are you feeling?" Paula asked, concerned.

Monica came and stood near the women. She took a piece of pie that Faith had just sliced and began sampling it. She smiled warmly at Faith and squeezed her shoulder in a way that let Faith know she had set aside her differences with her.

"You should feel great with all the attention you're getting," Monica said. "And even though you lost your baby, you have Elijah. He's busy, chatty and loud, but sweet. I'm going to like having him for a nephew. Maybe he will take everyone's attention off me and my life." She laughed softly. "Gerard treats him as though he has been in his life all along."

Hearing Monica's comments, Faith's eyes misted. Gerard had taken to Elijah, and he didn't appear to grieve the loss of their baby as much as she did.

The telephone rang and sent Monica dashing for it, leaving Paula and Faith alone.

"Don't mind her," Paula said. "She doesn't know what she's saying. You know how seventeen-year-old girls think." She placed a comforting hand on Faith's shoulder.

"I'm being too emotional. I can't seem to shake these blues," Faith said.

"You've been through a lot these last few weeks to make you that way," Paula said. "It's going to get better, dear."

Just then, the guys burst through the back door and passed through the kitchen to the living room.

Elijah came near Faith and eyed the slices of pie that were set on a serving tray. "I want some," he said with glee.

Faith stared at him. "We're going to serve it in the living room. Go in there and have a seat so can eat all together."

Quietly, Elijah ambled away.

Once they had settled in the living room with their desserts and were watching yet another game on television, Paula, who sat beside Rufus, said to him, "Faith told me she's going back to work tomorrow."

Rufus eyed his daughter. "Are you up to going back?"

Looking surprised at this bit of information, Gerard sat on the floor beside Elijah and stared at Faith.

"I'm more than ready. I've rested enough. Work is what I need now. I'm sure the beginning of holiday shopping will keep my mind busy," Faith said.

"Maybe tomorrow will be too much for you. I'm sure Tasha is more than willing to hold things down for you another day or so," Paula suggested.

"Yeah, she's right," her father agreed, looking concerned. "Fabulous will survive a couple more days without you. Take time to adjust to what has happened, Faith."

"No, there's no need for me to lie around feeling sorry for myself. That's not me," Faith said, feeling Gerard staring at her.

There was an awkward silence.

Paula looked at Rufus and Gerard. "After you guys finish eating, I want you to help me get those boxes of Christmas decorations down from the attic. I want to get started on them tomorrow. You know how I like being the first one to put my holiday cheer in the neighborhood."

Gerard said, "I'll be more than happy to help you, Paula. Elijah can help too. I'm sure he'll get a kick out of seeing all those fancy decorations you have."

"Help me take these things into the kitchen, then we can go up to the attic," Paula said to Gerard and Elijah.

Rufus rubbed his stomach. "You go on. I'll help later. I'm too stuffed to move at the moment."

Gerard, Elijah and Paula vanished into the kitchen with the dishes. When they could be heard thumping up the stairs to the attic, Rufus went and perched on the arm of the chair where Faith sat. He draped his arm around her shoulder.

"Are you really ready to return to work? Why tomorrow?" he asked.

"I'm be okay, Daddy. I need to get back to my life," she said, smiling appreciatively at his concern.

He stared at her. "You can't fool me, sweetheart. You can smile all you want, but those gorgeous eyes speak volumes to me. You walked around all smiles but with no sparkle when we lost your mother. Like all those years ago, I wish I could say or do something to help." He pulled her against his side and patted her back gently.

His caring touch caused Faith to embrace him and sob against his chest.

"Go on. Let it out. Losing someone is never easy." He cupped her chin and tilted her tear-streaked face toward him. "I love Paula a lot, but I still think of your mother," he whispered to his eldest daughter. "She was a terrific woman, a good mother. She was my first love and will always hold a special place in my heart. I was so sad when she left us that if I hadn't had you, I don't know what would have become of me. Remember, your mother told me to look after you." He took a deep breath as though he was releasing the painful memories of those days. He rubbed Faith's arm. "You've been through a lot recently. I can imagine it hurts, but that's life. It's one big roller coaster of emotions. But you truly have someone to love in Gerard. You can survive it all. That young man loves you. And that son of his, well . . . he's a fireball of energy, but he's all right. He has no trouble getting along with us. He seems to enjoy being with us. I kind of have the feeling he's been passed around a bit too much by his mother. The child said some things that led us to believe he's been living on too many broken promises from her. He could really benefit from the kind of love and respect you and Gerard have and can give him."

Faith listened carefully, but she still resented Iris's thoughtless intrusions on their life.

Her father broke her reverie by wiping her eyes with his handkerchief. "You're going to be okay," he encouraged. "You and Gerard will have plenty of kids." He grinned and tweaked her nose.

Though she knew her father meant well, his comment that they would have more kids wasn't consoling, especially since she had wanted so badly the one she lost.

Arriving home later in the evening from the Thanksgiving dinner at her parents' house, Gerard helped Elijah get settled in for the night. Faith went into the kitchen to put away all the food Paula insisted she take with her. Once she had done that, Faith settled in the den to watch television.

Gerard joined her on the sofa. "Elijah is worn-out. He had a ball with your family."

"I'm glad he did," she said, flipping the channels.

"He asked about Iris," Gerard said, sounding apprehensive. "Can you believe she didn't even take the time to call him? I checked our answering machine to see if she left any messages while we were out, but there were none."

"That doesn't surprise me. She was probably off partying with those hip-hoppers and her man, Legend. It only shows me how much she wanted to be done with him," Faith said. "How did you explain her not calling?"

"I told him Iris was thinking of him and was too busy working to call. I said she'd probably call within the next couple of days," Gerard said. He took her hand and held it. "Alone at last. It's been the best day we've had since—" He didn't know how to finish his thought.

Though she had no interest in the movie she

had found on television, Faith kept her eyes focused on it. She felt like a stranger to Gerard, and she resented the fact that he had been concerned only about his son's well-being. She felt as though he wasn't feeling the loss of the baby as much as she was. Elijah had been his comfort, she assumed.

He'd been wrapped up in making sure the boy had been entertained and happy for the day. She had been cordial to his son. Yet she couldn't keep from wishing he wasn't with them. She figured she and Gerard could have had a chance to share their grief privately.

Gerard broke into her thoughts by touching her face and turning it so she would look at him. "Are you sure you can deal with the store tomorrow?"

She closed her eyes to savor the warmth of his hand, yet she couldn't bring herself to express to him the love in her heart. In her anguish, she wanted to punish him for allowing Iris to push Elijah into their lives. Withholding her affection and not letting him into her thoughts was her way of reprimanding him. Throughout their relationship, Gerard loved her interest and the way she showed her love to him with secret looks, kisses and touches for no reason other than to show how happy he made her.

Shifting her head to avoid his display of intimacy, she said, "Dr. Wells told me she saw no harm in my returning to work. In fact, she thought it would be good for me."

Sitting forward and giving her a kind look, Gerard said, "I've said this before, but I get the feeling you don't think I'm being sincere when I say I'm as saddened as you are over losing our baby. As soon as we can, I'd like to attempt to have another kid. I know how important it is to you. Elijah has told me he'd love to have a sister or a brother. He wants plenty of brothers and sisters," he chuckled.

She wished she could show more enthusiasm, but she couldn't. She felt a tinge of guilt for not being glad Elijah had become so attached to Gerard and her even though she hadn't put forth much of an effort with him. She sat forward with tears glistening in her eyes.

Frowning, Gerard asked, "What now?"

Standing to leave, she looked down at her husband. "You have a son. I lost my child." She walked away from him.

"Faith, don't walk out like this. We must talk," he shouted. "I'm tired of you playing drama queen."

Freezing, she turned toward him.

He bounded from the sofa and confronted her. "What do you want from me?"

Fuming, she said, "I want our life back. I don't want to be anyone's stepmother."

Gerard's chest swelled with disappointment. "Well, it can't be that way. I'm a package now who comes with an eight-year-old son. When are you going to stop moaning and groaning about this? Faith, you got to show me all the love you professed before this situation came up. I can't make this marriage work alone." His veins stood out in livid ridges.

Covering her weeping eyes, Faith hung her head briefly. She and Gerard were headed into their first shouting match. She lowered her hands and lifted her face with its fallen features. "I'm beginning to wonder if this marriage stands a chance," she said caustically.

"I can live with what destiny has blown our way. You're the one who's acting like a spoiled brat," he said in a huff.

Faith's eyes flashed with anger. "How dare you speak to me that way? Is this the man who claims to love me? If you were in my shoes, you'd probably resent this as much as I do. I still can't believe you let Iris just breeze into our lives and dump her son so she can do what she wants. We're the ones stuck raising a child she obviously doesn't want to be responsible for or love as dearly as she claims. And I certainly don't want to look after him. I feel as though both of us are being used."

"That's not so," he said. "She is only trying to do the right thing at last. I believe Iris loves Elijah."

Faith grew angrier with Gerard defending Iris. She glowered at him and said, "Face it, Iris doesn't love anyone but herself. I feel sorry for Elijah, but don't expect me to fall in love with him." As soon as the words left her mouth, Faith realized they weren't alone. She glanced at the doorway and there stood Elijah in his pajamas, looking hurt and confused.

Gerard turned to where Faith's attention was drawn. He rushed over to his son and knelt before him. "What are you doing out of bed, young man?"

Elijah's bottom lip quivered. "I heard you fussing," he said in a trembling voice. He gave her a saucer-eyed stare. "My mom does love me, doesn't she? Why doesn't Faith like me?" He wiped his tear-filled eyes with the sleeve of his pajamas.

Gerard turned a cold look on Faith; then he said to his son, "Sure, your mother does love you. And Faith—Faith isn't feeling well since her return from the hospital. Let's get you back to bed. You and I have big plans tomorrow. I don't want you to be worrying over what you heard Faith and me saying," he said as he directed Elijah back to his room.

Another flicker of guilt coursed through her. She hadn't meant to hurt Elijah's feelings. Her issues were with Gerard and the way he had allowed Iris to manipulate him. She exhaled deeply and decided not to agonize over the argument. She had to heal her heart from the miscarriage. She didn't wait for Gerard's return from Elijah's room. There was nothing left for them to say.

On the way to their bedroom, she caught a glimpse of Gerard lying on the other twin bed in his son's room. That night Faith slept alone in her bed, fearing for her marriage.

CHAPTER ELEVEN

Gerard was relieved that he had made it through Thanksgiving without going insane. He had been caught up in a whirlwind of emotions. He had gone from being a man who had the fantastic love and attention of his hot, sexy wife to a man who had married a stranger. He had become a father who had gained a son and lost a baby.

"Where are we going?" Elijah asked, seeing his father pull into the parking lot of Jefferson High School. He had left the bank early to pick Elijah up from the baby-sitter's house.

"We're going to a basketball game to see the team Mr. Rufus coaches," Gerard said, loosening his necktie.

Gerard hadn't spent any real quality time with Elijah. The past week had been one of the most hectic he had ever known. It could have been easier if Faith had been supportive of him, he thought.

"Can I play basketball, too?" Elijah asked, unfastening his seat belt.

"Sure, you can. When I get some time, I'll show you some moves on the court," Gerard said, reaching over and touching the boy's head. "Come on, little man. Let's go see how Mr. Rufus's team is doing."

The nearly packed gym of rowdy teenagers was humid and had the smell of sweat. Holding on to Elijah's hand, Gerard checked the scoreboard and saw that the game was nearing the last half. He waved to Rufus before he and Elijah took seats in the bleachers.

Just as Gerard and Elijah had settled down, they were joined by Monica.

"Hey, brother-in-law. What's going on, kid?" She tickled Elijah playfully. Then she sized Gerard up. "You look like a college scout, dressed in that suit," she teased him.

Gerard studied the play that was being executed by Rufus's team before he responded. "Elijah and I haven't been home. We've run a couple of errands and had a bite at McDonald's." He looked at Monica. "I'm surprised you're at the game."

She shrugged. "You've got jokes," she deadpanned. "Just because Ahmad got tossed off the team for the next couple of games and I'm not allowed to see him doesn't mean I have to stop living," she said icily. "I have your wife to thank for my lack of a social life at the moment."

"I know you're not feeling sorry for that guy."

"You don't know. No one understands him the way I do. Ahmad has a lot riding on his dream," Monica said.

"Dream or no dream, you shouldn't allow him to manhandle you," Gerard warned.

Remaining silent, Monica crimped her mouth with annoyance and flashed a glance his way.

"Monica, you probably have plenty of other guys who want to take you out," Gerard said. "No reason for you to waste your life with someone who could fill it with confusion and heartache."

Monica gave Gerard a frigid look. "Like the way you've done my sister?" she asked. She jumped to her feet. "See you later, Elijah—brother-in-law." She descended the bleachers to join her girlfriends as Jefferson won by three points.

Her sarcasm annoyed him, but Gerard chased it out of his mind. He knew Monica had a lot to learn about life before she could judge him and his marriage.

Standing, Gerard spotted his father-in-law beckoning him. "Okay, son, come on. There's Mr. Rufus."

"Where?" Elijah enthused.

When Gerard pointed Rufus out in the midst of a small crowd, Elijah took off down the bleachers.

Gerard laughed at his son's enthusiasm. He was more than pleased that Rufus had welcomed his son into the family without hesitation. Rufus was a good-hearted and fair man. Gerard hadn't ever heard anyone say a negative thing about him. Elijah ran up, and Rufus greeted him with a bear hug that made the boy giggle with delight. Gerard wished he had his camera to capture the moment. By the time he reached the pair, he heard Elijah telling Rufus of his interest in basketball.

Gerard greeted Rufus with a pat on the shoulder. "Good game, man. Your boys are all right," he said.

"Thanks. I worried how we'd do without Ahmad, but we're okay. We're all better off," he said briskly, businesslike, referring to Monica. "My boys tried to give it away a couple of times. Had me shook for a minute." Rufus laughed heartily. "Our little man is telling me he wants to learn the game. Says he's never played. We're going to have to do something about that."

"I was telling him I was going to have to get him on the court and show him some basic moves." Gerard placed his hand on his son's head.

Rufus pointed to a guy who was carrying a bag full of basketballs. "Go over there and tell that guy I said to hand you a ball so you can bounce it a couple of times and get the feel of it. I've got something to speak to your father about."

As Elijah took the ball and bounced it, trying to imitate the players he had seen, Rufus stood with his arms folded and Gerard jammed his hands into the pockets of his slacks. Though both men wore pleasant expressions, it was obvious neither was truly content.

"How's Faith? I've spoken to her a couple of times and she keeps telling me she's fine, but I know she isn't," Rufus said.

Gerard rubbed the back of his neck and stared forlornly at Rufus. "To be honest with you, I don't know what to expect from her anymore. I love her, but she treats me as though she's done with me."

"She's put up that wall, huh?" He shook his head. "I'm worried about her. It took me years to crumble it when I married again."

"You're her father, her blood. She had no choice but to work it out with you," Gerard said.

Rufus stared at Gerard, smiling wryly. "It wasn't easy, man. Faith gave me and Paula a hard time. You would have thought we had committed some crime by falling in love and getting married. She and Paula are cordial to each other, but sometimes I still see jealousy in Faith. I have three women to deal with, and I have to be careful that I'm giving all of them the proper attention." He smiled. "Sometimes I feel as though they're keeping a scorecard on me."

Rufus glanced at his watch. "I've got to get back to my boys, but let me say this before I go. I went through this business of Faith being angry and treating me and Paula as though we were enemies. In my opinion, Faith never really got over the loss of her mother. They were close, and Faith was so young when Clarice left us." He cleared his throat. "I loved her mother dearly. I thought she'd be my one and only love. When she died, I drank to deal with my grief," he confessed. With a deep breath, he continued, "I didn't talk out my feelings with my daughter the way I should have, but I didn't know what to do or say to make her feel better when I was suffering myself. The only thing that kept me going in those days after Clarice's death was the fact I'd promised Faith's mother I'd take care of her and make sure she got a college education and turned into the kind of woman who'd make Clarice proud."

"Faith is an amazing lady. You did a good job of keeping that promise," Gerard said. "I was attracted to her because she's not only gorgeous, but smart and charming."

"Just like her mother. Yes, she is," Rufus said with affection. "When I married Paula and had Monica, Faith believed I was going to love her less, not have any room for her in my life. Can you imagine that? Looking back, I wish I had reassured her more of my feelings for her. I just assumed that, by her being older, she would just fall in step with all the positive changes in our lives. Both of us were like lost souls after her mother passed."

Gerard grew pensive. He knew Faith still resented Paula at times. It was probably where all her resentment toward him and Elijah had derived from, those unresolved issues tied to her mother's death.

Elijah ran up to his father. "Did you see the basket I made?"

Gerard had been so engrossed in his conversation with Rufus and with his thoughts that he had missed it. He stared at his father-in-law, feeling guilty for not having seen it.

"I saw it, Elijah," Rufus lied. "Give me five." He held out his hand to be slapped by the boy. "You keep practicing. You'll be a star player one day."

Elijah's brown face lit up with a proud grin.

"Look, you guys, I have to go and talk to my players before they leave. They're probably sitting waiting for me to tell them how spectacular they were, but I can't stroke them too much. They might get lazy on me, and we won't get that regional championship they deserve." He knelt before Elijah. "Have your old man bring you by on the weekend. We can rent some movies and eat some buttered popcorn."

"Yeah!" Elijah enthused.

Gerard grabbed his father-in-law's hand and shook it hard. "Thanks for the info. It's opened my eyes to the reason for Faith's attitude. I've got my work cut out for me, convincing her that we're going to be okay if she gives me the chance."

Rufus slapped him on the back. "You're a good man, Gerard. I'm sure you can work it all out." He hustled to the locker room.

"Can you buy me a real basketball tonight?" Elijah asked, staring up at his father as they made their way out of the gym.

"Not tonight, partner. Traffic is probably bad near the toy store. But how about us getting one early tomorrow morning? We'll even get you a hoop for the driveway, too," he said. "It'll be an early Christmas present."

As they sauntered out of the near-empty gym, Elijah did a celebration dance that made Gerard laugh.

Outside in the school parking lot, Monica leaned against her car, talking with Ahmad.

"I don't need this stress in my life," Ahmad told Monica, standing close beside her with his hands jammed in the pockets of his jeans. "It's the middle of the basketball season. How dare your old man treat me this way and expect me to transfer to another school? I won't get the love or the respect the way I do at this school where I have a right to be." He paced a bit with frustration. "I told the coach everything was cool between us. I apologized for what happened." He slouched against the car.

Monica leaned against him to snuggle up to his long, comforting form. "It's going to be all right. Maybe once my dad thinks that you and I aren't seeing one another, he'll back off and let you finish the season. I don't like sneaking around to see you, but if that's what we have to do, we'll do it until the tension settles." She gazed up at him and smiled. "How about a kiss? I've sure missed being with you."

"It's been tough," he said, wrapping his arm around her shoulders and giving her a lingering kiss that was followed by an endearing embrace from her.

Their privacy was invaded by the appearance of Cleo, a senior who had been out to capture Ahmad's affection.

"Oh no, Ahmad. I know you aren't playing me already. We haven't been together but a minute and you're out here sucking on her face."

Monica stepped to Ahmad's side and held on to his waist. She was confused by what she was hearing. Also, she was afraid of the rough girl who she knew lived in Ahmad's neighborhood. Cleo had been suspended for cursing out a teacher and fighting another girl over some gossip she claimed the girl had started.

Ahmad draped his arm around Monica's shoulders. "Cleo, I'm not trying to hear you. There's nothing between us."

Cleo stood with her hands on her hips. "There was plenty between us last night and several other nights in my bedroom. Don't get brand-new on me," she warned him.

"Ahmad, what is she talking about?" Monica asked, hoping there was no truth to what she was hearing.

Taking a confrontational stance before Monica,

Cleo said, "You're being replaced, that's what I'm talking about. Ahmad doesn't need a snooty girl like you in his life. He needs a 'round-the-way girl to make him happy."

Monica clung to Ahmad. "Let's go. Come on and take a ride with me," she said to Ahmad, turning away from Cleo to unlock her car.

Just as she had turned away, Cleo jumped on Monica's back, took a handful of her long hair, and tugged on it until Monica squealed from the pain.

When Ahmad went to get Cleo off of Monica, Cleo released her and began attacking Ahmad like a wild woman. She cursed him out loud and went for his face with her long nails, raking the skin until she left four long bloody lines.

Touching his bloody face, he went to Cleo and began shaking her.

Cleo grew wilder and began voicing all the promises he made to her and spoke of the intimacy they'd shared.

Ahmad drew back his hand to slap her, but security ordered him to halt his action and took hold of him. He struggled against the man. "I never told you I loved you, tramp," he shouted over his shoulder. "Stay out of my life, Cleo."

A crowd gathered at the scene. More school security appeared to clear the parking lot of the melee that was brewing.

Cleo got into Monica's face. "He'll never be yours," she said in a spiteful tone. "He's my man. He's mine, and don't let me or my friends catch you with him, or you'll be sorry." Cleo leaped at Monica, spittle flying from her lips, her face twisted with ire.

Monica's eyes flashed with anger. "I'm not afraid of you. You don't own him."

"Neither do you," Cleo retorted before a security guard came for her and hustled her back toward the building where Ahmad was being led too.

When Gerard saw that Monica was involved in the high school fracas, he took hold of Elijah's hand and made his way through the curious mob of students to get to her. He found her leaning on the hood of her car, sobbing and trembling with humiliation.

"Monica, come on with Elijah and me," Gerard urged her. "We'll see to it that you get home safely." He took hold of her shoulder and squeezed it. "That was Ahmad, I assume," he said quietly.

She turned to Gerard and fell upon him and cried.

Gerard comforted his new sister-in-law with a hug, and he was pleased to see that Elijah was sensitive enough to give his aunt a hug as well.

"I've been such a fool," she said in between sobs. "I believed everything he said to me. I thought I was the only one he loved." She sobbed and then paused. "I was willing to accept him with his child, but Cleo is too much."

Gerard knew this was the wrong time to lecture her. He said, "Leave your car here. Your dad or I will get it later. Relax. We'll take you home, where you can think things through and pull yourself together."

Gerard slipped his arm around her waist and Elijah took her by the hand. They led her away to Gerard's car, which was parked on the other side of the lot.

Once Gerard got Monica safely home to Paula, he was sure Monica's mother would fill Rufus in on everything that had happened while he was with his team.

Gerard hoped that the evening's events helped to show Monica Ahmad's true character. With her realization, she wouldn't waste any more of her emotions or thoughts on him. He remembered that once Iris had shown him how selfish and inconsiderate she was, he had no trouble getting over her.

Fabulous helped Faith to forget her predicament at home. Between waiting on customers and stocking the shelves, Faith didn't have a chance for a pity party. She'd called her friends Nicole and Sydney and asked them to stop by the store on Saturday to take a look at the donations she had gotten for the Morning Has Broken clothes bank from other stores in the mall.

It wasn't until six o'clock that evening that the two ladies appeared. Their timing had been perfect, since there were only a few customers in the store. Nicole and Sydney were impressed with the quality of suits, blouses and even shoes that had been handed over to Faith for their charity.

"Plus sizes," Nicole exclaimed. "We really needed things for our larger-sized women. We've got make sure to get thank-you letters out to the stores as soon as we can." She held up a navy blue suit and picked up a striped blouse that would match it perfectly. "I know a woman in a halfway house whom this would be perfect for," she said. "She's going for a clerical position at the community college."

Nicole was caught up in rummaging through the clothes, but Sydney studied Faith.

Faith felt Sydney's eyes on her and met her gaze. "What?"

"You have no business doing all of this work. You just lost a baby. You should be taking care of yourself more," Sydney said.

"I'm all right. The work for the foundation and with Fabulous has been therapeutic. A busy mind with busy hands doesn't have time to think."

"But you should take time to grieve," Nicole said. "I've been there. Remember, I miscarried last year. I know about grief. I grieved hard. You know, my husband and I have been trying to conceive since that loss, but we haven't been lucky yet. I believe we want it too much—that's why nothing has happened."

"Then, of course, I lost a baby, too," Sydney added. "Mine was two years after my first one was born. Though I had a child, I had baby lust. I needed another baby. I wasn't satisfied until I was able to get pregnant with my second kid," Sydney said. "You and Gerard should be able to start working on another kid right after the first of the year."

"I don't know about that," Faith said.

"Why not?" Sydney asked, preparing a cup of tea.

"He and I have too much to do, too much to resolve to consider another child. After all, there is Elijah, and the issues that has brought between us. He takes up most of Gerard's time," Faith said dryly.

"Do I hear a hint of envy in your voice?" Nicole said.

Faith laughed nervously. "No, you don't. Why should I be envious of an eight-year-old boy?"

Sydney and Nicole gave her a knowing look.

Faith leaned against a wall, looking forlornly at them, then she said in a barely audible voice, "Okay, I'm going to be honest with you two. I know I can confide in you. I'm embarrassed by all this chaos in my life. I've been walking around like I'd married royalty who was going to give me this ideal life, then he and I learn after all these years he has this secret son by his ex-wife." Faith, briefly became lost in thought. Then she said, "I feel kind of ridiculous for being so idealistic at my age. I never expected all my dreams of a happy life to be smothered by the curve fate has thrown my way."

Seeing how distraught Faith was, Sydney went to her side. "You have nothing to be ashamed about. All of this was out of your control."

Nicole was nearby too. "That's right. These things happen in marriage, in life."

Faith moved away from them toward her cluttered desk, where she dropped down into her leather chair. She was holding back tears she didn't want them to see her shed. "Easy for both of you to say. You don't have to live through this mess."

"How is it a mess? Don't tell me Gerard doesn't want the child," Sydney said.

"No. It's not him. It's me. I'm the one who doesn't want the boy staying in our home. What's wrong with me wanting some privacy with my new husband? Is it so wrong for me to have wanted to be the first and only one to give my husband a child, and a son at that? I grew up sharing my father with Paula, and now everyone expects me to share Gerard with his kid all while wearing a big grin." Her voice broke, and she lowered her head and began crying softly.

Sydney went to Faith and began rubbing her back. "You need time to get used to all of this. Is Gerard's son bratty?"

Accepting tissues from the box that Nicole handed her, Faith said, "He's an energetic boy. He makes a lot of noise. But I really haven't had that much to do with him," she admitted. "He goes to Gerard for whatever he wants and when he wants to talk. He probably can sense I'm not into him."

"Sounds to me as though you're the bratty one," Nicole said.

"Nicole," Sydney chided with a whimsical smile.

"Well," Nicole said. "Someone should say or do something funny about now."

Faith's cheeks had turned rosy from her crying. She sat sniffling.

"Relax, Faith. Your hormones are all crazy," Sydney said. "Your body has to get readjusted from the miscarriage. To top things off, you've been working like a maniac. I believe you returned to work too soon and have been working too hard, plus doing volunteer work with the foundation. Take it easy, girl. If you're married and have kids, you're going to have to learn to laugh at some things. Learn to lose a few battles, kiddo. It'll make you humble real quick." She chuckled.

"I wish you had told me all of this before now," Faith said with a hint of a smile.

Mischief lit Nicole's eyes. "If we had told you all the stuff that goes on after you get married, you wouldn't have believed us. The way you glowed whenever you and Gerard were together, I have a feeling you thought your life with him was going to be without the usual chaos."

"You've got that right. There are compromises,

and a whole lot of other things you won't want to do too," Nicole agreed.

"As long as you two love each other, you'll be able to get through this. You have to commend Gerard for falling right in step with fatherhood," Sydney said. "So what if you have to assume the stepmom role?"

"I don't want to be second to anyone," she snapped. "It's not fair. Gerard could have made her wait a bit longer before letting that child move in with us." Her words were full of fury. The agony consumed and twisted her delicate features. Her insides shuddered from all her negative thoughts.

A tense silence enveloped the room.

Nicole and Sydney were at a loss for words about their friend's ire. Silently, they continued to sift through the donated clothes.

Feeling ashamed for what she should have kept to herself, Faith couldn't apologize. She pulled out a rolling clothes rack and began to hang the outfits on it. "I can't wait to see the ladies' faces when they get a look at the great stuff we've gotten." Whirling around to her friends, Faith wore a forced grin, hoping to assure her friends she wasn't going insane.

"Gerard had to rescue Monica last night after the basketball game," Faith said to change the subject.

Looking at Faith with interest, Sydney asked, "What happened?"

"My sister met Ahmad after the game. Because of the awful incident with her—you know, the deal with him roughing her up that I told you about."

With concerned looks, both Sydney and Nicole nodded.

"Ahmad hadn't been able to play last night, and he didn't show up for the game either. Yet he met Monica in the parking lot, where one of his other girlfriends confronted him for being with Monica. Gerard said there was a big mess. The girl whom Ahmad had been stringing along was loud and embarrassing, and she even attacked Ahmad, then came after Monica. Thankfully, security put an end to it.'

"Oh my goodness," Nicole said. "It's a good thing Gerard was around."

"I was glad he was there with Elijah. They'd gone to see the game," Faith said. Then she sighed. "I hope this will put an end to things with Ahmad for good this time. From what we've learned from the women who come to Morning Has Broken, sometimes a woman has to be humiliated by the man she thinks she loves to come to her senses."

"What a shame for girls to be getting into a fight over a worthless guy," Sydney said. "But that's high school, I suppose."

"I'm sure you showed your gratitude to Gerard for looking after your sister," Nicole said, grinning.

Faith smiled slowly. "Well, I felt he deserved a

hug and a kiss for his kindness. My father called and said he was glad Gerard was family and knew how to stick together as one."

"Exactly, girl," Sydney said.

"The Lord is trying to show you what a good man you got," Nicole said.

Faith sighed and nodded, knowing that despite the deal with Monica, she still wasn't able to accept the change in her life.

CHAPTER TWELVE

A few evenings later, Gerard had an unexpected visit from Alex. He had come to check on his friend, whom he hadn't been able to catch up with by telephone.

"What are you doing out this way, man?" Gerard asked, opening the door for his friend.

"I didn't have any cold beer, and I know I can always count on you to have some," Alex said, making his way to the fridge to help himself to a brew. "Where's your son?"

"He's in his room. He's probably asleep by now. I'm glad you came by. There's been a bit of action in the family. The other evening when Elijah and I stopped by the high school to see what Rufus's team had, we ended up in the middle of a scuffle between Monica, her boyfriend and the boyfriend's secret woman." Gerard went to the fridge and got himself a beer too. "Monica had a bad scene with that guy Ahmad she wasn't supposed to be seeing anymore."

"What did that punk do to her?" Alex asked.

"Embarrassed the hell out of her and showed her what a waste of time he's been for her."

"Man, he's a shame. I've been following Ahmad in the sports pages. According to the media he could be all that, but he has a cocky attitude that could keep him from being the next big sensation." Alex drank from his beer.

"I don't know about this kid. I understand he's had it rough, but still, it doesn't give him the right to walk around with a chip on his shoulder and act as though he's a star already. He could begin a whole new life with the skills he has, but that attitude of his is going cause him to block his blessings."

"I hear that. I've seen it happen too many times, man," Alex said. "Monica is okay, though, isn't she? He didn't put his hands on her?"

"Not this time. I wasn't going to let that happen."

Frowning, Alex said, "You mean he's been smacking her around?"

"There was an incident where she and he had an argument and she had bruises on her arms."

"I hope Monica's old man set him straight," Alex said, looking concerned.

"Rufus thought he had taken care of things between them. He's trying to get Ahmad to transfer. In fact, he was suspended from school and the last couple of games. He wasn't even supposed to have been on the school grounds when Monica was with him in the parking lot."

"Well, I hope she learned her lesson to leave that scrub alone," Alex said, shaking his head.

"I think Monica finally gets it with what happened that night," Gerard said, taking a big gulp of his beer.

"How's the little lady—your wife?" Alex asked. "I haven't seen her since your unexpected addition."

Gerard sipped his beer. "She's returned to work at Fabulous. She stays busy there or with that foundation."

"Has she warmed any toward Elijah?" Alex studied his friend.

"She's polite, but I wish she would be more than that. She's stingy with her words with me, and I'm lucky if I can get a kiss or a hug from her. When we're in bed at night, she turns her back. I feel blessed when I wake in the morning and find her cuddled up to me in her sleep," Gerard said. "Grab a bag of chips off the counter. Let's go to the den and find a game on television." He left the kitchen with Alex following. In the den, the two sprawled on opposite chairs.

"Your love life is on ice, huh?" Alex asked, feigning a shiver.

Gerard nodded. "It's not funny, man. She hardly lets me get near her. And since she lost the baby three weeks ago, she has all the more reason for me not to touch her intimately. Every now and then, I get lucky and catch sight of that sexy body of hers coming out of the shower wet or see her in the midst of dressing or undressing. Either way turns me on—drives me wild. But that's as good as it gets for me. Oh, I forgot to tell that she did show me her appreciation for being there for sister by rewarding me with a hug and a brief kiss that left me hungry for more."

Alex chuckled, but cut it off when he saw his friend wasn't laughing with him. "I'm not making fun of you. But you've got to laugh at how far Faith is taking this. Women can be so unreasonable."

"I don't know what to do. I don't want to go through Christmas with Faith acting like an ice princess toward me and especially toward Elijah," Gerard said. He had slumped in his chair and was looking worried. "I want Elijah to have some fun and feel wanted. He's not getting that feeling from Faith the way he should. She merely tolerates him. No child should grow up feeling that way."

"I can't believe the way Faith has shut down on you. It's so unlike her," Alex said.

"We're going to have to have some give-and-take in this marriage, or I'm afraid she and I will be headed for trouble," Gerard said. "Elijah has Christmas vacation next week. Faith mentioned to me she was planning on taking a few days off to clean and decorate the house for the holiday." He paused. "She doesn't know that I'm going to have to leave Elijah with her. His baby-sitter is going out of town. Then I'm going to need her to take him to the pediatrician for a physical. I want him to be set up with a physician here in case he gets sick in the next few months."

"I sure would like to be around when you assign her these duties." Alex chuckled.

"It's not going to be that big of a deal. I need her, and it's time she stepped up to support me. I would do the same for her, because she is my wife."

"Good to hear you're taking charge as head of your household, dude."

"Faith has got to learn we don't have time to act like kids. We have a child's welfare to think about now," Gerard said in a no-nonsense tone.

Alex rubbed his head, looking at his empowered friend. "It would be a sin to see you two lose what you had. Shoot, you and Faith had it going on so good you had me thinking about settling down," he admitted. "Maybe after Elijah returns to his mama, Faith will have a chance to rethink her actions and regret her behavior."

Gerard finished off his beer, crushed the can and tossed it into the trash.

"I've heard nothing from Iris. I don't know what her next move is going to be. I have this gut feeling Elijah will be here much longer than we expected," Gerard told Alex. "Besides, it's not like Elijah is going to be out of my life then. Faith has to learn to accept that Elijah is my son if we're going to be together," he said testily. "I miss the woman I fell in love with. The one who stole my heart and soul, and made me love her with her sweetness, her intelligence and that hot sensuality. I really don't want to lose what I had. But she's going to have to stop treating me and my son as though we're enemies."

Alex shook his head. "Sounds to me as though Iris couldn't wait to get rid of Elijah. I think you're right when you say he'll be here a while."

"That doesn't pose a problem for me. What gets me is the fact that she won't take the time to call him. Elijah asks about her, and I can tell he misses her sorry behind. I only wish she'd call and say something to him. I know it will mean a lot."

"If she plays the disappearing act on the little man, she's going to regret it. She'll be the one who misses out," Alex said. "It's a shame the way they let any woman be a mother."

"I really feel bad for him," Gerard said. "His own mother has ignored him, and Faith won't take the time to get to know him. All he has is me. I won't desert him," Gerard said with conviction. He jumped to his feet. "I've got to check on him and make sure he's resting comfortably." He had to leave the room before his emotions got out of hand. He was filled with misery over the way his son was being treated.

When Faith was able to leave the store counter and head to her office, she was surprised to find Monica at her desk, listening to her iPod. The two hadn't been alone and hadn't talked the way they had since Faith had revealed Ahmad's cruelty and caused an end to Monica's relationship with her boyfriend.

"What a pleasant surprise," Faith exclaimed. "I've been calling and checking on you. I was hoping for a visit from you. I didn't think it would take so long before you were ready."

Monica unhooked her earplugs and smiled. "Mom and Dad told me. I guess I was too ashamed to admit you were right."

"You should never be ashamed to come to me."

Monica shrugged, looking as though she was holding back tears. "I'm sorry for the way I treated you over the thing with Ahmad."

"Apology accepted. I'm just glad you've come to your senses. Gerard told me everything. I'm grateful you had a chance to see for yourself what kind of guy he is." Faith went to her small fridge and retrieved a bottle of water, opened it and took a generous swallow. All the while, she studied her sister and smiled. "You missed getting freebies, didn't you?" She laughed softly to uplift the mood.

"You always kept me hooked up with some sweet clothes." Then Monica's laughter faded and a single tear streamed down her face.

Faith went to her and hugged her. "It's okay now. You thought you were in love with him. There's always one man a woman makes a fool of herself over." Releasing Monica, Faith studied her face. "It's over now. A lesson learned. You're out of that relationship before something worse could have happened." Faith took a seat on the edge of her desk, near Monica. "As far as I'm concerned, you and Ahmad wouldn't have found happiness."

The sight of Monica's cute features marred by the pain of a woman who'd been used filled Faith with empathy. Tenderly, she brushed Monica's shiny hair. "You've got to learn to guard your heart better. Don't ever let a man abuse you verbally, and certainly not physically. That isn't what love is."

"I'm beginning to understand that. But you know, Ahmad and I did have some good times. Though I know I won't have anything else to do with him, I still have leftover feelings for him." She shook her head. "Isn't that crazy?"

Faith sighed. "Yeah, it is. But that's life. Your feelings will fade in time and only be bittersweet memories. You're becoming a woman who can't flick her emotions on and off like a light switch."

Monica wiped a tear away that had streamed down her face, and managed a smile. "How are things with you and Gerard? Mom and Dad are worried about you two. I overheard them saying they're afraid if you don't become more understanding, you're going ruin your marriage. You can't lose him. He's become my hero."

Standing quickly, Faith hid her inner turmoil

from Monica. She walked to her file cabinet and busied herself there.

"You know, I *had* taken your side on this situation before I understood what the deal was. Mom explained it to me. Gerard had no control over anything that's driving you two apart. You've got to make it right with him. You're married to one of the finest and sweetest men in Bellamy. Anyone who sees him with you can see he's in love with you. You have what I dream of having someday. Don't let Gerard get away. You two belong together."

Faith chuckled nervously at the younger woman who was trying to give her advice. Eyeing her sister, she paced a few steps, looked at her and said, "Don't worry about me. Things will work out one way or another." She shrugged.

Before anything else could be said, Monica's cell phone made a melodious ring. She glanced at the display on her phone and flipped it open. "Essence, where have you been? You won't believe who asked me for a date today. Where are you? Home? I'm at my sister's store. Don't go anywhere. I'll be there in thirty minutes so I can fill you in on everything." She flipped the phone shut. "Got to go, Faith. I'm glad I came by. I've missed you." She rose from her seat and headed for the office door. Then she halted, turned and rushed to Faith and hugged her. "Count on me to baby-sit Elijah for you and Gerard when you go

173

to that fabulous charity event I've been hearing about."

Returning her embrace, Faith said, "That's mighty kind of you. Remember, I'm always around for you. I love you, and don't ever forget that."

Stepping away from Faith, Monica's face was radiant with joy. She waved good-bye and was gone.

Returning to the floor of the store, Faith wished she had a guarantee for Monica's happiness and the romances in her life. But no one knew better than she that, when it came to romance, there were no guarantees for complete harmony in a relationship.

When Faith arrived home from work that evening around ten thirty, Gerard greeted her warmly. She returned his hello and headed into the kitchen for a bite to eat. She had decided on heating up a microwaveable low-carb frozen dinner. She had picked up her mail on the way to the kitchen. She sat at the table and began opening the bills she'd received.

Gerard appeared and leaned over to kiss Faith on the cheek, hoping as he always did recently that he would receive tenderness instead of the polite affection she returned.

"Tea?" he asked, taking the kettle to the faucet.

"That would be wonderful," she said absent-mindedly, studying a bill.

Setting the kettle on the stove and turning on the heat, Gerard said, "Elijah begins his Christmas holiday next week. No school until after the New Year. I overheard you telling Paula you were planning to take a few days off to get the house decorated and cleaned for Christmas."

She brushed her hair from her face to tuck it behind her ears, and stared at him.

"Elijah's baby-sitter is going out of town for a few days. It would be great if he could sleep in a couple days—hang out with you. He'd be a big help to you."

Faith settled back in her chair and gave him a "get real" look.

Despite her negative body language, Gerard continued, "And I've scheduled a visit for him to the pediatrician for a physical. You shouldn't mind taking him there. It's with Eva Carey at two o'clock on Monday."

He stood with his arms folded and leaned against the counter with an expression that showed he was ready for a confrontation. He saw Faith chew on her bottom lip thoughtfully, and expected her protest.

"Okay, I'll help you out," she relented.

Gerard was stunned by her easy acceptance. He rushed over to her and hugged her appreciatively. "Thank you, baby. He won't be a bother. I can't wait to tell him that he'll be able to stay home and not be hustled out of bed next week."

He had planted a kiss on her forehead and was set to kiss her lips, but the microwave beeped to signal that her meal was ready.

She shrugged him off. "My food is ready, and I'm starved."

He watched her pad barefoot to the oven and pull out the hot meal. Ripping away the cellophane, she said, "I'll only be able to help you for three days. I need to be at the store after that."

"Fine. I'll make other arrangements for the rest of the week. Elijah might be able to stay at his friend Joe's house. I'm sure that his classmate's mother will welcome him. She's a stay-at-home mom."

Faith grabbed a fork out of the cutlery drawer and began eating her meal, standing up with her back to her husband.

Feeling dismissed, Gerard left her alone in the kitchen. Just as he pushed through the kitchen door, he heard the tea kettle whistling as if letting off the steam that he felt from Faith's aloofness, but he kept it in check.

Chapter Thirteen

The Monday morning before Christmas, Faith was awakened by Gerard, who was dressed for a day in the office, shaking her shoulder gently.

She rubbed the sleep from her eyes and sat up in bed. "What time is it?"

"Seven thirty," he answered. "I've to get out of here and to work. I have a long day ahead of me and some planning to do first thing this morning. Elijah and I had a long talk last night, and I told him not to give you any trouble. He vowed to help you with whatever chores you had for him to do." Gerard's hand rested on her thigh.

"Good. We should be fine," Faith said, yawning, without any enthusiasm. She didn't confess to him that she had slept restlessly, thinking of how she was going to manage being alone with Elijah. He was a stranger to her. She remembered how easy it had been take care of her younger sister when she was growing up. But she had heard

from her friends what a handful of mischief
young boys Elijah's age could be. This had filled
her with anxiety. How was she going to discipline
the boy without coming across as the wicked
stepmother? she mused. Also, she felt as though
Gerard was testing her to see how she would treat
his son on her own. She wondered if the en-
durance of her nerves with Elijah was a measur-
ing stick for their relationship, which appeared to
be growing more fragile with each day.

"The appointment with Dr. Carey is at two o'-
clock. I've already filled out the forms they gave
me the other day I stopped by the office. It's only
a general physical. Call me and let me know how
things go there." He glanced the digital clock on
Faith's nightstand. "I've got to go, babe, or else I
won't beat that morning rush-hour traffic." Smiling affectionately, he kissed her on the cheek.
"Good luck." Then he hurried out the room,
snatching his suit jacket.

Falling back on the pillow, Faith stared at the
ceiling and she thought of the day that lay before
her with Elijah.

Eva Carey had only been practicing for three
years. Yet she had managed to have the reputation
of being one of the favorite pediatricians for the
kids of Faith's friends and other people in Bellamy. Eva was warm and friendly with her tiny
patients. She dressed in colorful cartoon-character
scrubs. She was a lovely woman Faith's age. Faith

was glad Gerard had decided to make her Elijah's physician.

"Hey, Faith, how are you today?" Dr. Carey said, entering the examining room. Elijah was sitting on the end of the table in his briefs with a paper gown. "I see this young man, Elijah Wynn, is scheduled for a physical. I spoke to your husband the other day. He's quite fond and proud of this young man who has come into your lives." She winked at Elijah.

"Yes, he is," Faith said. "He's Gerard's pleasant little surprise."

"How are you feeling, Elijah?" Dr. Carey asked him.

"Fine, ma'am," he said shyly.

"Then we'll just take a little look around."

Eva began looking into Elijah's eyes and checking his throat. Then she continued her examination.

Faith took a seat nearby and crossed her legs and noticed how wide Elijah's eyes with anxiety had grown. She smiled to ease his tension, but he seemed too busy worrying about what the doctor was going to do. Gerard had told her that Elijah had a fear of getting a needle. Though they hadn't talked much on the drive, he had been concerned over whether or not he was going to get a needle.

"I hope you plan to attend the charity ball," Faith said, watching Eva check Elijah's chest with a stethoscope.

Removing the earpieces of her instrument from her ears, Eva said, "Yes, I'm looking forward to it.

We've all worked so hard on this thing. And it's been a while since I've attended a fancy ball." She grinned.

"I'm glad to hear that. I hope you have you a handsome date to share the evening with."

Eva picked up Elijah's chart and began to scribble. She grinned at Faith. "Well, I do. Alex Washington has asked me to be his date."

Faith's mouth fell open. "Alex, huh?"

"It's only an evening. One date," she said. "Don't go make it into something more. I'm aware of Alex's rep with the women."

Faith knew Alex had a crush on Eva, but she didn't relate this information to Eva. She was staying out of her business, because she certainly had enough of her own to be concerned with.

"I'm sure Alex is going to be on his best behavior. He knows you're not the usual sure thing he's used to canoodling with."

"Like I say, it's only an evening out for me to relax and have some fun." Eva shrugged. Studying the papers Gerard had filled out, she glanced at Faith. "This young man seems to be in good shape. The only thing left is to do some lab work on him. We're going to have to get a urine sample and prick his finger to find out if everything else is A-OK."

Faith saw Elijah sit upright, and his eyes widened. Faith thought she heard him gulp.

"I'm going to send my nurse in to take care of that. I'll give you guys a call if anything returns that's irregular." Eva turned to Elijah and touched him on the shoulder. "It was nice meeting you, young man." She turned to Faith. "Take care. I'm sure you and I will run into each other again with all the meetings we have for the foundation before the fabulous ball."

"Thanks, Eva," Faith smiled as the doctor left.

"I'm going to get a needle," Elijah whined with tears welling in his eyes.

Faith moved out of her chair and went to him. "It's not a big needle, hon. The nurse is going to prick your finger with a tiny needle. It won't hurt. I'm going to be here with you and you can hold my hand while she does it."

Elijah leaned toward Faith and reached for her hand.

Just then the cheery nurse entered with a tray that contained the things she needed to do the procedures.

Faith was touched by the way Elijah clung to her hand. She held his hand tightly and told him to relax while the nurse had to do what she had to. Once it was over, Elijah stared at Faith with a relief-filled smile.

In that instant, she clearly saw a resemblance to Gerard that further proved that there had been no mistake in the paternity test. It was evident that she had some changing to do. If she wanted her marriage to work with Gerard, she was going to have to do better by him.

"Can I put my clothes on now?" Elijah asked,

breaking her reverie. He hopped down off the exam table.

"Yes, you can," she said, handing him his things from the nearby chair.

By the time they'd left the doctor's office, Elijah was full of chatter, and he sat forward in the car tinkering with the radio for music he preferred over her mellow jazz station. He hit the power button, and the music blared so loudly that Faith shouted, "Enough, Elijah. Sit back and be still."

He did as he was told and looked out the window at the passing traffic.

As they drove along, Faith felt guilty for her impatience.

"Would you like to go by the bank to see your dad? You can tell him about your visit with Dr. Carey." She spoke softly.

He beamed at her. "Can we?"

"Yes, I'll call him from my cell and let him know we're on our way. I'm sure he'll be glad to see us."

Gerard was delighted to learn that Faith was bringing Elijah for a visit.

Elijah had been driven by the bank's headquarters, where his father worked, but there had been no opportunity for Gerard to show him the inside of his office.

Once they had parked in the garage and caught the elevator up to the second floor, where Gerard worked, Elijah burst into the bank the moment he saw his father standing at a teller's window with some papers.

When Gerard spotted Elijah, his face glowed. He turned away from his business at hand and knelt and opened his arms to his son, who came rushing up to him. He lifted the boy off the floor.

"How was that doctor's visit, my man?" Gerard asked his son, lowering him back to the floor.

Faith watched the two of them and the unmistakable love between them. She was amazed at the bond that had formed between them in such a short time. She envied them, because she still struggled with her feelings of envy and fear at sharing her man with this little boy.

She eased up on the two. "Everything went well. Eva said he appears to be in tip-top shape. She did some lab work on him and said she'd call if there was anything to be concerned with."

"That's sure good to hear," Gerard said without looking at her. He rubbed Elijah's head playfully. "Come on to my office, so you can see where I go and what I do all day." He took him by the hand and led him down a hallway toward his office.

Faith felt a pinch of jealousy. Her man hadn't even looked at her, nor had he greeted her with a kiss. His attention was strictly for his boy. She followed the two into Gerard's office. She couldn't remember the last time she had dropped by for a visit with him. Before Elijah had arrived, she would often drop by to see him and to share kisses with him behind closed doors.

Entering the office, Elijah headed straight for his daddy's plush leather chair. He made himself comfortable and set to swiveling back and forth.

Gerard stared at Faith, reached for her hand and pulled her toward him. "It hasn't been so bad, has it? He's something else." He kissed her lips briefly.

Gerard released her and went to where Elijah was, and showed him the great view he had of downtown Bellamy from his window.

While the two shared the view, Faith's eyes fell on a framed picture that sat on Gerard's desk beside the one of him and her taken when they'd become engaged. The eight-by-ten color photo was of a beaming Gerard with a happy Elijah sitting beside him. Gerard had his arm wrapped around his son's shoulders. She picked up the picture, which she'd had no knowledge of.

"This is really nice," Faith said, holding it up for Gerard as though he hadn't seen it. "When did you have this done?"

"He and I had that done at a department store in the mall one day while we were having a day out. You were busy working," he explained. "It's a good father-and-son picture, don't you think?"

"It's nice," she said, setting the picture back where it had been placed. She felt awkward not being included. But she knew she hadn't warranted a position in their life. Hadn't she made it clear to her husband she wanted nothing to do with the boy when he first arrived?

"We stopped by because Elijah wanted to see you. We'd better be on our way. I have to stop by the grocery store, and then I intend to get busy with Christmas decorations. I've talked to Elijah about helping me decorate the tree."

Gerard beamed at her. "That's great. I'd love to be a part of that too. Maybe we can take some pictures—for the family album."

At the mention of family, Faith cringed on the inside. If she had not lost their baby, her stomach might have a little bulge by now. It would have made her first Christmas with Gerard much happier and Elijah's presence more bearable. She glanced at the picture of Gerard and Elijah once more, and her heart ached. Did Gerard truly have enough love for more than one child? she wondered. Then she realized she should have been asking herself if she had enough for Elijah. She knew that if that door in her heart didn't open soon for Gerard's son, she wouldn't have that to worry about. She was certain that she would lose Gerard, and with him, all of her hopes and dreams for a future of happiness.

That evening Gerard arrived home a bit later than usual, because he stopped to do some shopping. He arrived with several boxes of Christmas lights to adorn the outside of the house. He told Elijah they would work on that the coming weekend. The Wynns' house would be the standout on their block, he told his delighted son, whose eyes lit with joy.

While Elijah dug in the bag to check out the colorful lights, Gerard turned at Faith and said, "Where's the tree?"

"It's in the garage. The man from the nursery delivered it a few hours ago," Faith said, pleased with the way he looked at her. "But before we work on that tree, let's eat this dinner I've cooked, before it gets cold. It's Elijah's favorite—hot dogs and beans."

Gerard walked up to her, kissed her and held her, laughing softly. "This really feels like home."

She surrendered to his embrace and held him close to share a brief tender kiss. Like him, she wanted this to feel like home too.

For the first time since Elijah had moved in, the three of them sat at the same table and ate dinner together. Sitting at the head of the kitchen table, Gerard was ebullient.

Faith got caught up in her husband's joy and laughed at the silly jokes he was telling Elijah. Gerard was amazing. He had managed to win the trust and love of this little boy who until weeks ago he had never known existed. Seeing him with the child only proved to her that he was born to be a father. She was proud of the way he had taken his responsibility, but she just couldn't stop wishing that she could have learned what a wonderful father he would have been with their child or children—ones that had come from their love.

That evening Faith pulled out her Christmas CDs and put them in the sound system to add to the mood. They'd decided to place the fresh pine tree in the living room window so that everyone who passed their house could see the beautiful decorations the three of them had done.

Once the tree was done and they'd turned on its lights, they insisted Elijah had to go to bed. He had already stayed up an hour past his bedtime. Gerard had him take a bath and get into his pajamas before he went to say good night.

"We all had fun tonight, didn't we?" Sitting on the side of Elijah's bed, Gerard adjusted the covers.

"Yeah, we did. I wish Mom could have been here. We never had a big tree like the one we got. Mom and I only had a small fold-up kind of tree that she'd set in the middle of our living room table." He rubbed his eyes with the backs of his hands. "Why hasn't she called, Dad? Do you think she's thinking 'bout me?"

"Sure, little man, she's thinking of you. You're her heart," he said to encourage the child. "She's probably been really busy. She's going to call before Christmas," he said, hoping Iris wouldn't turn his words into a lie. "Get some sleep, buddy." He turned out the lights and left his son.

Returning to the living room, he found Faith sitting on the sofa in the dark, her feet folded beneath her, staring at the lighted tree. Taken by the sight of her lovely regal profile, he stood feeling frozen in time by the desire he felt for her. His heart raced a bit, and he sauntered to the chair and sat beside her. Pulling her toward him, he wrapped his arms around her and proceeded to kiss the back of her neck and behind her earlobes. She squirmed and giggled with delight the way he knew she would. He took her onto his lap and began to lavish her with deep, passionate kisses.

Gerard's kisses were sweet and warming. Faith snuggled against him and was intoxicated by everything male about him, from his strength to the smell of his body and his urgent affection for her. Passionate heat settled at the bottom of her stomach and grew moist in her feminine core. She wanted him sexually, but wondered if it was safe to act on her desire because of the miscarriage. She had been so distant from Gerard, she hadn't bothered knowing for sure. She had to get her checkup from her gynecologist before she indulged.

Before she knew it, she was on her back on the sofa with Gerard on top of her, grinding against her and kissing her and touching her as though his existence depended upon her loving. She allowed him to remove her shirt and bra and to feast upon her breasts. His wet lips and insistent tongue sent a blaze of heat throughout her. It took everything in her to halt his ardent actions.

"Gerard, baby, we can't get too carried away. We can't have sex yet. Remember," she said in a low sensual voice.

He sighed with frustration. "No sex," he groaned. He sat up and pulled her up against him. He continued to fondle her breasts. "When is that visit with your doctor?"

"It's not scheduled until the week after Christmas."

"That seems like a long way."

Faith looped her hands around his neck. "Just think how great it will be when we get together."

"You're going to learn the true power of love when I can really get with you." He kissed her and laughed.

After that night, Faith and Gerard got caught up in the magic of Christmas. Once again they began to act like newlyweds. Gerard had even been able to get Faith caught up in getting Christmas gifts and wrapping them for Elijah "from Santa."

Filled with elation, she looked forward to sharing her first Christmas with Gerard.

Two days before Christmas, a large box was delivered by FedEx. Faith looked at the package and saw that it was addressed to Gerard, and it was from Iris. She took the package and placed it in their bedroom for Gerard to inspect when Elijah wasn't around.

After he was told of the package, he didn't open it until Elijah had gone to bed. He asked Faith to be with him to open the box, which he figured held Christmas gifts. Sure enough, there were several wrapped boxes inside. Then Gerard opened the letter and read the one page that had been enclosed.

While Gerard read the letter, Faith busied herself with tidying up their bedroom. She heard him crumple the letter, and noticed her husband's expression turning solemn.

"What did Iris have to say?"

"These gifts are clothes—designer outfits she and her man have chosen for him to keep him hip-hop-trendy, she said. She wants me to give him a hug and send her regrets for not being able to being to call or see him on Christmas. She intends to call me after Christmas and talk to Elijah then."

"What in the world does she have to do to keep her from at least calling her son? I overhear him asking you about her every day. He keeps waiting for a call or looking for a piece of mail from her."

Gerard sighed heavily. "Iris is making it hard. I'm doing my best not to make her appear as though she doesn't care for him." He got up off the bed, removed the box and walked into their closet to hide the gifts for Christmas, which was only two days away.

He reappeared and announced, "I'm going to watch television and have a beer."

Faith felt sorry for her husband as she watched him stroll out of the room looking miserable. Yet she knew he would manage to make Elijah have a pleasant Christmas despite his mother's thoughtlessness.

* * *

Like most stores that Christmas Eve Friday, Fabulous had been extremely busy with last-minute shoppers. When she left the mall that evening, she wasn't fatigued. She was thrilled to see that it had begun to snow lightly. The weather was perfect for the cozy evening that lay ahead of her at home. She and Gerard had a big night ahead, wrapping gifts and arranging the toys they had bought Elijah for Christmas.

"Can I go see if Santa came yet?" Elijah said loudly as he burst into their room at six o'clock in the morning.

"I'm sure he has. Let's go see what you've gotten." Flinging the covers back, Gerard hopped out of bed.

Faith sat up, grinning as she watched Gerard dash behind his son. She climbed out of bed and slipped on her robe to join them around the tree.

Entering the room, she saw Gerard hovering with a camera over an enthusiastic Elijah as the child ripped wrapping paper from gift after gift. He had received all the latest electronic games he wanted, as well as books and some sports equipment such as a football and a helmet with his father's favorite team colors. After Elijah had opened his gifts from Gerard and Faith, Gerard handed him the several boxes his mother had sent him.

"Mom was here," Elijah said, looking anxious.

"No, she sent these to you. You're always on her

mind. She said to be sure to tell you merry Christmas and that she would call in a few days," Gerard said, taking a seat on the floor beside his son.

With a smile, Elijah opened his mother's gifts. Inside each box were some really expensive clothes with a rich rapper's logo scrawled upon them. The boy seemed pleased. He wanted to wear one of the jogging suits his mother had sent to dinner at Faith's parents' house later, he told them. Then Elijah sat under the tree, examining the toys he had received.

Faith sat on the sofa, watching her husband reach under the tree to hand her a couple of presents from himself and from Elijah. He insisted she open them while he took pictures of her.

"Don't," she protested, chuckling. "I haven't combed my hair and my eyes are still swollen from sleep," she said as he aimed the camera.

"You look fine. Open Elijah's gift first. That would be the one wrapped in the the Santa paper."

Faith did as she was told.

Elijah came to sit near her with his hands on his knees, watching her.

Opening the square box, Faith discovered a large-faced watch with a dial that lit up and a wide black band.

She leaned over to Elijah and hugged him. "Thanks so much, sweetie. It's just what I need."

The boy looked awkward from the first hug Faith had given him.

"You're always busy and have somewhere to go. I told Dad this would help you be on time."

Faith felt a twinge of guilt for the truth the boy spoke. She had always made excuses for not being around him or at home to help care for him.

"Thank you," she repeated softly to him. "Now let me see what your father has gotten me." She proceeded to open the small box, with Gerard holding the camera on her.

The next gift made her gasp. There was a beautiful set of diamond earrings. She bolted from her seat and fell upon her husband, holding the earrings in the velvet box. She embraced him and he returned her warmth.

"Merry Christmas, my angel," he whispered and kissed her, wearing a smile.

"I expected coal in my stocking for Christmas for being naughty," she murmured against his lips as they ended their kiss. She leaned away from him and gazed into his brown eyes, her eyes turning misty with joy.

"Now that would have been an appropriate way for me to show my love for our first Christmas." He held her against him.

"I love you," she said.

"I love you more," he added, his eyes sparkling with his emotions. "I want you to wear those to that Black and Silver Ball, as you ladies called it in the invitations."

She removed herself from his embrace and

went under the tree to get the special gifts she had for Gerard and Elijah. She handed a big box to Elijah and one the same size to Gerard, along with a smaller one. She watched them open the big boxes, which held matching jeans and hooded sweatshirts for them to hang out in.

They were pleased with the outfits, which would give them a father-and-son look.

Elijah placed his gift under the tree and went back to playing with an electronic game he had gotten.

Gerard sat on the arm of chair to open the second gift. It was a gift certificate for him to get a plasma television from the electronic store in their area.

He grinned broadly. "Oh my, Alex is going to be jealous," he said. "He's going to want to park himself around here to watch all the sporting events with me." He went to her and kissed her. "Thanks, baby."

"I'm glad you like it," she said. "We'd better prepare breakfast. We have a long day ahead of us still. Come, Gerard, you aren't playing with Elijah's toys. You've got kitchen duty with me. I'm fixing French toast, bacon and eggs."

Gerard hooked his arms around her waist as they walked in tandem.

Faith giggled from his silliness, yet she was enjoying every moment of their first Christmas together. She refused to let the unsettled issues of Iris and Elijah stand in the way of the day.

CHAPTER FOURTEEN

The Thursday before the charity ball on New Year's Eve, Faith visited Dr. Wells for her follow-up exam after her miscarriage.

"Everything looks great," Dr. Wells told Faith after her examination. "You have the go to begin having sexual relations. I bet your husband will be glad to hear that."

"I'll say," Faith responded, thinking how ready she too was to begin a physical relationship.

"Well, this is perfect timing. What a way to start the new year. I can imagine you're ready to try for another baby, too." The doctor smiled.

"If that happens, it would be wonderful," Faith admitted, thinking how her life was beginning to feel the way it should as Mrs. Wynn.

"I'll look forward to seeing you soon," Dr. Wells said.

Faith smiled at the physician. "I hope you and

your husband will make the Black and Silver Ball this weekend."

"Of course, we're looking forward to it. We're going along with another couple who are good friends of ours too."

"Great. I'm sure you'll going to enjoy yourself. According to the plans of the committee, it's going to be quite an evening for our worthy cause."

"I can't wait. My husband and I both work so hard, we hardly have a chance to get all decked out and go dancing and to relax," Dr. Wells said. "Look forward to seeing you at the affair, lady." She left Faith to get dressed.

On her drive from the doctor's, Faith used her cell phone to call Gerard, who was at work for half a day. Elijah was spending the day with her father and Paula. The timing was perfect for them to get together intimately.

"I just left the doctor's office and I passed my follow-up checkup. She has given me the okay to have sex."

"An extra holiday gift," he enthused in a lusty tone. "I have a few things to clear up here. I should be home within the hour."

"Perfect. I'll be waiting for you, sweetie," she said in a sexy voice. Then she hung up. She grinned, and her body tingled with anxious anticipation of all the catching up they had to do in the bedroom. It was good to live in the house without tension. Faith attributed the return of the closeness between her and Gerard to the holidays. Things were good between her and Elijah. But she was tolerating him for her husband. She also knew that it wouldn't be long before his mother returned to pick him up. Then she would only have to deal with Elijah on the visitation days that Iris and Gerard would agree upon.

With Elijah living with his mother again, she and Gerard could once again focus on their life and their children, Faith thought.

Faith rushed home and showered quickly with her lavender-scented gel. She stepped out of the shower, slipped into her short terrycloth robe and headed into the bedroom. Surprised by the sight of her husband, she gasped.

Laughing at the surprised expression on his wife's face, Gerard said, "I didn't mean to scare you, girl. I wanted to be undressed and in bed by time you came out of your shower." He tore away his clothes and tossed them across the room.

"I wasn't expecting you for a while yet," she admitted. Once her heart stopped racing, Faith was pleased with his presence.

Once he was completely nude, he stood smiling proudly as though he were a work of art—a splendid statue—with his arms open to her.

She floated to him, palmed the sides of his face and began sharing heated kisses with him.

Gerard pulled open her robe and shoved it off her shoulders, causing it to drop to the floor. He slid one arm around her waist and cupped her bottom until she was flush against him.

While they were pressed together, Faith felt their flesh grow heated. She was also turned on the hardness of Gerard's throbbing member as it titillated her dewy core. As they strained and struggled against one another in passion, they nearly lost their balance.

Between nibbling kisses and urgent touches, Gerard lifted Faith off the floor. Her legs went around his waist, and she licked and teasingly bit his neck. He moaned, his face radiant from her hot-blooded antics. He made his way over to the bed, where they tumbled upon the middle of it, a tangle of arms and legs.

Landing on her back, Faith laughed with glee. Though Gerard was on her and had started weakening her by sucking gently on her nipples and licking her breasts as though they were honey-flavored, she managed to pull out of his embrace. She wanted to be on him, and he conceded. He lay on his back, staring at his wife as she buried his ramrod-straight penis within her with a sigh of utter pleasure. Bracing her hands on his chest, she proceeded to rock back and forth as though she was in a rocking chair.

Admiring the heavenly look upon her face and the glow of sweat on her honey complexion, he took hold of her breasts and thumbed each nipple while undulating his body to her hypnotic rhythm.

Faith opened her eyes to meet the loving gaze of her man, and took a breath, knowing she could no longer restrain the mounting desire within her. Feeling the blood sizzling in her veins and the cresting of her climax, Faith swiveled her hips faster and harder upon her husband's essence. Soon she was moaning loudly with her eyes squeezed shut. It was evident she had reached her climax, and it was astounding. Her thighs quivered in the midst of their shared bliss, and Gerard sat up, delivering her all that he could as love burst within her.

At the end of their encounter, he pulled her down upon him and locked her in his arms.

Faith's body was full of ecstasy and a feeling of peace that she'd missed. Feeling drugged from their love, she exchanged nibbling kisses and endearing words with her husband. Before they drifted off into a lovers' nap, they uttered *I love you*s. Then they slept in a spooning position for the next couple of hours.

New Year's Eve, the Black and Silver charity ball for the Morning Has Broken Foundation was resplendent with elegance. It was definitely going to be the talk of the town, and an event that would be repeated.

Faith's friends Sydney and Nicole were as tickled as teenagers at a prom with their handsome husbands dressed in tuxes and clinging to their sides. The champagne was flowing, and the room was filled with gorgeous arrangements of white and red roses. Along with a wonderful gourmet dinner, there was a marvelous band with a lovely and dulcet-toned female singer who was nothing but the truth.

The moment that Gerard and Faith entered the ballroom, people stared at them as though they were royalty. Gerard was movie star–fabulous in his tux, and Faith looked like an angel who needed only wings. She was dressed in a glamorous strapless light blue silk gown with a tasteful split up the front that revealed her great legs. Her hair was upswept to reveal the twinkling diamond earrings her husband had given her for Christmas.

They were followed by Alex Washington and Dr. Eva Carey. With the enchanting Eva on his arm, dressed in an eye-catching red gown, Alex wasn't as cocky as he normally was. He acted as though he was on his best behavior to impress the woman who, he had declared to Gerard, could make him settle down and live a contented life with only one woman. He had to convince Eva Carey of this, though. He had a reputation for being a love-'em-and-leave-'em type, but he intended to let Eva know he had good intentions toward her.

Much to their delight, Gerard, Faith, Alex and Eva had been assigned the same table for the evening. When Eva and Faith left the guys alone to check on the brief program they had planned, Gerard and Alex had a chance to speak.

"Man, I can't believe I'm here with Eva," Alex

said, rubbing his hands together. "She is fine in more ways than one. She was reluctant to accept my invitation. I had to use all my powers to get her to come with me. And it's been worth it. She is so different from all the women I've been with. She's bright, cultured and just a sweet woman."

Gerard squinted at his friend playfully. "Man, you're been bitten by the love bug, and bad too. It sounds as though you're ready to give up your playa's card, buddy."

"If I could have Eva as my lady, I'd burn it," Alex said with conviction.

"Wow, you're real," Gerard said. "I wish you well. I hope this evening is the beginning of great things for the two of you."

"Thanks, man. I blame you for the condition I'm in. I'm happy you and Faith pulled your thing together. You two are back to being the most sickeningly in love couple I know," he teased. "She's glowing, you're glowing. It can only mean that everything is back the way it should be for newlyweds."

"It's been indescribable. With a little patience, I knew I would win back the woman I'd married." Gerard smiled. "She and Elijah are doing good, but I'm hoping for better. The most important part, though, is that she's trying with him instead of ignoring him. I can't ask for more under the circumstances."

"The last couple of times I visited you, I noticed she hasn't been acting like the ice princess," Alex said. "Elijah doesn't seem to be afraid to ask her for things or to sit up under you when she's in the room around you guys."

"It was wild for a while, but, like I said, it's getting better. If only Iris would call the boy, I would be a happy man. Every child likes to know his mother cares."

Alex nodded. Then his eyes drifted over to the corner where Faith, Eva, Sydney and Nicole hovered, discussing last-minute details from legal pads.

"I wish Eva would bring her pretty self back to the table. I can't wait to have a dance with her—the only gentlemanly reason to have my arms around her and hold her." Alex got a dreamy look in his eyes.

"You need to keep some of that to yourself," Gerard said, chuckling. Gerard glanced toward the door and saw Rufus and Paula. "There are my in-laws. Let me go speak to them," he told Alex, getting up.

Faith saw her folks too. She and Gerard met up with Paula and Rufus at the same time. Gerard wrapped his arms around Faith's shoulder the moment they came before Rufus and Paula.

Rufus held his wife's hand and grinned. "If I didn't know better, I would think I was at your wedding reception from all the affection you two are showing each other."

"Rufus, leave them alone. It's a beginning of a

new year. They have every right to be happy," Paula said. She looked chic in a gold gown.

"You look amazing, Paula," Gerard said.

"Thank you. Monica helped me picked this out. She claimed I'd look really hot in it." She laughed softly.

"And you do, lady," Rufus agreed. "I have to stay close by you so no one will steal you from me."

They all laughed.

Faith showed her father and Paula to their assigned table and introduced them to the other couples there.

The band had gone from playing an upbeat song to a popular soul ballad.

As Faith looked around the room for her husband, he surprised her by slipping up and taking her by the hand.

"I was looking for you," she said, giving him her best smile.

"That's good to know." He lifted her hand above her head and made her twirl. She beamed as the soft fabric of her gown swirled around her. Then he pulled her to him and fell into the slow rhythm of the song.

"Everything has really turned out splendid. Everyone loves the ambience of the night. The committee and I are considering making this an annual event. We've done well with ticket sales and there have been private donations—generous ones handed over this evening too," Faith told her husband as excitement danced in her light brown eyes.

"I'm pleased, baby. But let's enjoy this dance." Gerard pressed his cheek against hers and held her to him until she could feel his heart thumping against hers.

Closing her eyes, she let her husband lead her on the dance floor to the romantic song with the beautiful lyrics. This evening was heavenly, and she wanted to relish every moment along with all her other holiday moments.

Dancing with her husband humming softly and sweetly in her ear, Faith felt for a while as though she and he were the only two people who existed in the room. When he kissed her on the earlobe, she shivered, and her heart felt as though it sparkled. She could have swayed and stepped in his embrace against his strong body forever.

Near the end of the very successful evening, Faith was pleased to hear that the Morning Has Broken Foundation has raised nearly fifty thousand dollars from the ball, from private donations and from the continued sales of their charitable items. Feeling euphoric, Faith and Gerard sat around drinking champagne and eating strawberries and chatting and laughing with friends. Faith heard her cell phone ringing in her purse. Reaching for it, she stared at Gerard and shrugged . She knew it could be no one but Monica, who was spending the night to baby-sit Elijah.

"Hello," Faith said. "How are things going?"

"Elijah is asleep and I've been watching television," Monica said. "I hate to mess up your groove, but I thought you'd like to know that Iris Wynn called looking for Gerard. I told her you both had gone out for the evening. It was a few minutes ago when she called. She was talking slurred like she was high or something, and she asked to speak to Elijah, but I told her he was sound asleep."

"What?" Faith said loudly enough to get the attention of Gerard, who was standing beside Alex on the other side of the table from her.

"She didn't like it. She cursed. But she told me she'd call you guys sometime tomorrow. She's in town for a few days and she wants to see her baby, she said," Monica explained. "I thought you'd like to know about it. She kind of bothered me with her attitude. I didn't know if she'd have second thoughts about coming by and trying to cause trouble."

"I'm glad you called. Gerard and I will be home as soon as we can. Don't let anyone in. If she shows up and tries to cause trouble, you call the police. We'll be there soon." Faith hung up the phone and went to Gerard to relay confidentially what Monica had said.

"What is Iris up to now? She could have called before she showed up in town out of the blue this way." Gerard's brow furrowed.

"We need to get home now. No telling what Iris

may do. I don't want Monica to have to deal with this alone," Faith said.

On the drive home, Faith nor Gerard had much to say.

During the holidays, she and Gerard had begun to work through their difficult times and get close the way they had started their marriage. Who knows what confusion Iris is about to cause now that she's in town? Faith thought. Could it be that she had come for Elijah? Faith stared at her husband as he drove, and could tell he was worried. Gerard had grown quite attached to Elijah, and she knew that he was going to want to know every detail of what the flighty woman had in mind for their son.

Faith had a feeling that Iris's arrival was going to mean disaster.

CHAPTER FIFTEEN

Faith wanted Gerard to tell Elijah his mother was in town. However, Gerard hadn't mentioned a word to his son. Fortunately she hadn't shown up the night of the ball. But Iris was too unpredictable for them to be unprepared. If she didn't follow through with getting in touch with them, Gerard didn't want to risk disappointing the boy. He'd spent most of the morning waiting anxiously for a phone call or visit from Iris. True, Iris claimed she had only wanted Gerard to keep Elijah for a few months. But, now that Iris had returned, Faith could see he wasn't ready to give up his son. Faith knew he had come to love him and wanted to keep him in his life. Since the holidays, things had improved in the Wynns' home. Elijah seemed to have been adjusting well in Bellamy, in school and in making friends. It was for this reason that Gerard had told Faith that he believed

Elijah could be given a more stable upbringing than Iris could offer him.

It was after two o'clock in the afternoon when Iris arrived at their house.

Hearing Iris cheerily and loudly greet Gerard at the door, Elijah dashed from his bedroom and ran to meet his mother with a hungry hug.

"My goodness, you've grown since the last time I saw you, boy," Iris said, grinning and hugging her son.

"Mom, I missed you. Why didn't you call like you promised?" Elijah asked, staring up at his mother, who wore large designer sunglasses.

Gerard placed his hands on his son's shoulders. "Elijah, let's invite your mom in to have a seat. Then we can all talk about what we've been doing."

Standing in the background, Faith checked Iris and could sense melancholy in the woman who was dressed from head to toe in trendy casual wear of jeans, sweater and a long, black leather coat.

Elijah took his mother by the hand and led her into the living room. Gerard took her coat so that she could sit down with Elijah.

Faith made her presence known. "Hello, Iris. I hope you had a great holiday," she said, trying to be cordial to the unpredictable woman.

Iris removed her glasses and offered Faith a weak smile. "Hi. Yeah, it was good," she said with a lack of conviction.

"Can I get you something?" Faith offered.

"I'd like a drink. I'd love a cold beer," Iris said. She settled back in her chair, with Elijah sitting as close to her as he could.

"How about a soft drink, Iris? I drank the last beer last night," Gerard lied.

Iris shrugged. "Okay, a soft drink will do." She rubbed Elijah's head affectionately.

"I'll get it for you," Gerard said, leaving the ladies alone.

Staring at Elijah cuddling to his mother, Faith could see how much he had missed her. She thought of how amazing children could be. Regardless of a parent's shortcomings or insensitivity, a child managed to love his or her mother unconditionally.

"So, Faith, how do you like standing in for me?" Iris asked cockily. She smoothed the side of her hair.

"Believe me, I haven't been trying to take your place. I know he'll only have one mother," she responded curtly. "Elijah and I get along. He and I have learned to be friends." She smiled at Elijah.

Relieved when Gerard returned with a glass of soda for Iris, Faith quietly slipped from the room. She sensed Iris had something she wanted to discuss with Gerard concerning Elijah. Since she wasn't his parent, she felt the three of them needed to be alone, and that she would be an intruder on matters that had nothing to do with her. She excused herself and went into her home office to attempt to look over the fiscal reports delivered that morning involving the monies from the charity ball. Just as she had begun tapping away on her calculator, Gerard burst into the room.

"She wants Elijah to spend the day with her. She insists on taking him to that new animated movie that opened on Christmas," he stated. He appeared stressed.

"You don't think it's a good idea for him to go off with his mother? He looks as though he would love it," Faith responded, staring at Gerard, who had taken a seat on the desk near her. "Let him go. He's been so disappointed that she hasn't called him since she dropped him off with you."

"Something is going on with Iris to bring her here. I asked her about her Legend, and she didn't want to talk about him. I asked her about the career thing, and she said it could be better and then she changed the subject." With a pensive expression, Gerard folded his arms. "Something doesn't feel right. She's staying at a motel and she's driving rent-a-car. She claimed she felt guilty for missing Elijah's first Christmas away."

"What's a couple of hours, Gerard?" Faith asked. "You don't have sole custody of him, so you don't have any other choice but to let him go." She stared at Gerard intensely. "Did she say anything about when she was going to resume her responsibilities for him?"

"Not a word. From her conversation, she seems to be passing through for a few days." He got up and paced the room. "You're right. We're only supposing to be baby-sitting him for now. But I'm going to call my attorney first chance I get Monday and clear up what my responsibilities and visitation rights are over hers," Gerard said. He stood and walked slowly out of the room. "It's cold and rainy outside. I'm going to make sure he's wrapped warmly for the weather."

After Gerard left, Faith settled back in her chair. She thought this was going to be the beginning of Iris's high jinks with Gerard and Elijah. She had given Gerard enough time to love and know his son, Faith reasoned. Now that they had bonded, Iris would probably attempt to use Elijah as a token to manipulate Gerard for her benefit in some way. Faith sensed that Iris was shrewd. Iris had used Gerard when they were younger, and Faith doubted she was above doing it again. Iris was one of those women who used men to get whatever she needed. It was probably the reason why her precious man Legend wasn't with her, Faith mused.

Once Iris had left the house with her son, Faith stood near Gerard at the living room window, watching Elijah hop and skip to the car with joy.

"He'll be fine," Faith said, placing her arm around Gerard's waist and resting her head on his shoulder.

"I sure hope so," he said. He opened a piece of paper he had clutched in his hand and studied it.

Faith could see that Iris had written her latest

cell phone number and the number of the motel near the interstate where she was staying. Gerard folded the paper, slid it into the pocket of his jeans and walked away from the window after Iris's car had disappeared down the street. He went into the living room and settled in front of the television. He picked up the remote and flipped through the channels. Then he jumped up from his seat and grabbed his coat.

"I'm going out to visit Alex and see what he's up to," he called to Faith, who had returned to her office. Then he was gone.

Faith knew Gerard wasn't going to be content until Elijah was returned home. She had seen the worry clouding her husband's eyes. It had only taken him a few weeks to show what a loving and caring father he could be. She should have been encouraged, but despite the facts she couldn't stop wishing she had been the only mother to their children. She was growing more comfortable with Elijah, but she knew she wouldn't be satisfied until she had a child with Gerard. Maybe then she could open her heart to Elijah and be more accepting of the situation.

"Iris is back, man. She's taken Elijah off to a movie," Gerard said, marching past Alex to enter the house. His leather jacket was damp from the heavy downpour of rain that had started as he had gotten halfway to his friend's place. The weather echoed his mood.

"Good afternoon, my friend," Alex said. He followed Gerard into his kitchen, where he headed for the fridge for a can of beer.

Popping open the can, Gerard took a big gulp. "I have a bad feeling about this, but there wasn't anything I could do. Elijah was so glad to see his mother. I've been trying to reassure him that she would come. Bam! She showed up last night, calling the house late while we were at the dance. Monica spoke with her and said she sounded as though she had been drinking or something."

"Sounds as though the lady has issues," Alex said, leaning on the counter and picking an apple from the bowl there to munch on. "It's just a movie, man. She hasn't come to take him home, has she?"

"She only wanted to visit Elijah," Gerard said.

"I don't know why you're so worried. He's lived with her all of his life. He seems to have turned out pretty good," Alex said. "She's his mom. She won't do him any harm. You're worried about him because you've grown close to him."

"I love him. He's my boy and I won't have Iris snap him up out of my life."

He finished off the beer, crushed the can in his hand and flung it into the trash can.

"Calm down, Gerard. Relax. It's going to be cool. I'm sure once the movie is over, she'll probably load him up on all the fast food he wants and return him to you safe and sound. Iris isn't going to take him. She can't move around or party the way she wants with Elijah in tow." He took a couple more bites of the apple and dropped the core into the trash. "Hey, last night was great. That Eva is amazing. She has enchanted me." Alex grinned and placed his hand over his heart.

His action got a smile out of Gerard. "Did you enchant her, too?"

"I don't know. She is quite a lady. Eva was fun to be with, but unlike most of the women I date, she has a very busy life. And what's worse, she's heard rumors of me being a 'bad boy.' She has no time to play dating games like a teenager, she told me. She would like a relationship, but she'd like to spend what free time she has with someone who is not out to play her."

"She is serious, and she has let you know what she wants. Are you ready to be the kind of man she wants?" Gerard asked.

His face was full of strength and confidence. "I want this woman. She's what I need in my life. I am willing to do whatever I must to convince I'm for real."

Gerard chortled at his playboy friend.

"Why you want to make fun of me? Okay, I've met my match. It was bound to happen. I'm not getting any younger. I want to grow old with someone to love me too."

"Go for it," Gerard encouraged, hiding his smile behind his hand. He couldn't believe his friend had been smitten so badly.

"It's good to see you smile. I'm glad that seeing a player go down has taken your mind off your troubles." He went to Gerard and shared a high five. "Have another beer. I could sure use one. I have a big challenge ahead of me dealing with that bit of sweetness named Eva Carey."

Gerard and Alex spent the next couple of hours watching ESPN and voicing their opinions on the sports news being reported.

When Gerard's phone rang, he reached for it in the pocket of his coat, which lay on the chair near him. From staring at its caller ID, he saw it was Faith.

"Yeah, baby."

"Gerard, you have to get to the hospital. Iris and Elijah were in auto accident. She called, crying." She paused. "Elijah was hurt—"

"No! Please, dear God, no!" Gerard's eyes were transfixed with horror, and he jumped to his feet.

"It's awful, I know. Get Alex to drive you to the hospital. I'll meet you there," Faith ordered in a sympathetic tone.

Reacting to Gerard's panic, Alex questioned him. When he heard the news, he wasted no time in grabbing his coat and leading Gerard out of the house to drive him to the hospital.

Faith was the first to arrive at the emergency room at the hospital. She was greeted by Iris, whose eyes were haunted with fear.

"It happened all so fast," a frazzled Iris said. "The rain started coming down hard, and I had

215

no way of seeing the car that came crashing into us from out of nowhere, nearly totaling the car."

Impatiently, Faith took hold of Iris's arm. "What about Elijah? How is he?"

"The paramedics bought us in. Poor baby was crying and in pain." Her voice quivered with emotion. "There was a lot of blood on his face, and he complained of his arm hurting—" Iris slumped her shoulders and burst into tears.

Suddenly Gerard hustled up on them with Alex hurrying behind him.

"Where's my son? Who do I have to speak with concerning him?" He ignored Iris's tears and insisted upon an answer.

"A doctor is in with him now. They said they'd be with me as soon as they had examined him." Irish grabbed the sleeve of Gerard's jacket and held on as though she wanted comforting from him.

He shrugged her away from him, went to the reception desk and questioned the clerk in a no-nonsense manner. She left her station, went in the back and returned shortly with information that didn't ease the anxiety on Gerard's face.

"The clerk said the doctor will be out to talk with us," Gerard said.

Iris went to Gerard, fell upon him and sobbed.

Though Faith was as worried as they all were, she couldn't help but take exception to the way Iris clung to her husband. She tried not to linger on the situation. Her feelings weren't important at this time. Elijah was what mattered, she reminded herself.

Alex stepped up to Faith and offered a weak smile. "Can I get you some coffee or something?" He placed his arm around her shoulder in a friendly manner.

Staring up at Alex, Faith said, "I'm fine. I hope Elijah isn't seriously hurt."

Alex nodded with understanding. "Everything is going be okay."

"Let's pray that it is," Faith said, watching a fretful Iris whispering to Gerard.

After a while, the emergency room doctor appeared. "Mr. and Mrs. Wynn," Dr. Henry announced as he approached.

Both Iris and Faith got up and followed Gerard to meet with the doctor. Following him to a corner of the emergency, Faith took hold of her husband's hand.

"The good news is that your son will be fine. Elijah had a deep cut right above his eye. We stitched it and it should heal without incident. Being as he was unconscious when he was bought in, we'd like to keep him for a couple of days to see how he progresses. Also, Elijah sustained a fracture to his right arm. It's being set now and he will wear a cast until it's mended. We're making arrangements for a room."

"Can we see him?" Gerard asked.

"Yes, you can. He's a bit groggy, but he will be fine," Dr. Henry reminded them. "Nurse, will you show them where the boy is?"

Gerard released Faith's hand and strutted off behind the nurse, with Iris trailing close behind him.

Faith hesitated.

"Aren't you going?" Alex asked, placing a hand on her shoulder.

"I'm not his mother, so I'll wait and get Gerard's report." Irrationally, she felt rejected, although no one had denied her admission. Faith couldn't meet the look of concern she saw in Alex's eyes. She took it for pity, and she sure didn't want any of that. She walked to the cafeteria for a cup of coffee. She returned to the waiting room before Gerard did.

When Gerard returned from seeing Elijah, he was relieved. He rushed up to Faith and embraced her.

"He's doing good. He's going to be fine." He was obviously pleased now that he had seen his son.

Alex patted him on the back. "Phew, I'm grateful to hear that. We were all given quite a scare. Where's Iris?"

"He wanted her to stay with him until he was moved to his room. I'm going back to be with him, too," he told Faith.

He didn't invite her to see Elijah and she was hurt. She and Elijah had gotten quite friendly with each other, and she'd come to care for him.

But obviously she didn't fit in this equation now that his mother was present.

"Faith, I know you don't want to sit around the hospital with us. Go home and relax. I'll be home once Elijah is transferred to his room and settled in for the night."

"So you're dismissing me." Faith's mouth pinched with annoyance.

"No, I'm not." Gerard's brow knitted. "I was only considering your well-being. Iris is here to do what she should as his mother."

"Fine, Gerard. I'm going home to leave you alone with your family." She whirled away from him and marched out of the emergency room to the parking lot.

Gerard didn't try to catch up to her, but Alex did.

"Wait. Let me see you to your car, Faith," he said, walking in step with her. "Gerard isn't thinking straight. Elijah's well-being is the focus of his attention. Don't take this personally. You know the man loves you."

But the explanation only made her feel worse. This was what she knew would come of letting Elijah into her life. He would always be a priority, with Iris somewhere in the midst as though she was still Gerard's wife.

As she reached her car, the veins at her temple throbbed with the beginning of a headache. She stared at Alex. "I do take any woman entering my life, and causing my husband to dismiss

219

me as though I don't count, as personal," she fumed.

"Iris will be gone again. Believe me, you can count on that," Alex said, trying to console her.

"She can't leave soon enough for me. I've only known her a short time, and each time she appears, she brings nothing but trouble." She started her car. "See you later, Alex. Thanks for your help."

"No problem. I'm hanging around to drive Gerard to pick his car up at my place. If you need anything or just want to talk, I'm available," he reminded her as she backed out of the parking spot.

A dull, empty ache gnawed at her soul. Everything had been falling into place for them so positively until Iris appeared unexpectedly. Faith was beginning to open her heart and to let Elijah in. Yet, with Iris around, Faith was sure that Elijah's mother was going to say or do something to set back her attempt at a relationship with Elijah. She could see that Iris was trying to maintain two worlds: one where she could still be the center of her son's attention, and another where she could go off and party as though she didn't have a responsibility in the world.

With a sigh, Faith thought that this was what her future held: a life of Iris dropping in and out of Elijah's life whenever she felt like it. Faith expected that after a while Elijah would use his mother to manipulate the love Gerard had for him in order to have his way. In other words, if

Gerard wouldn't relent to whatever Elijah wanted or needed, he would probably threaten to go off and live with his selfish mother. If Elijah was going to be in their lives, Faith had to let Gerard know he had to make it clear to Iris that she couldn't use the boy to benefit her selfish needs. What a way to start the New Year, she thought. Her eyes misted over with furious tears. She anticipated being more aggravated the longer Iris hung around Bellamy.

CHAPTER SIXTEEN

It was way past eleven o'clock that night when Faith heard Gerard returning from the hospital. Lying in bed, Faith had been mulling over the current situation and wondered how much more chaotic it could get. She noticed that it was taking Gerard some time to come to their room. She figured he had stopped in the kitchen for a drink or was relaxing in front of the television before coming to bed. After all he had been through, maybe he needed some time alone, she reasoned. Then she heard her husband having a conversation. Curious, she got out of bed and stood at her bedroom door to hear what was going on. She heard Iris's voice. What in the world was she doing at their house this time of night? Faith pulled on her robe and, with a spurt of adrenaline coursing through her veins, she went to the kitchen, where she found Gerard and Iris. He was preparing sandwiches for them while Iris sipped a beer.

"Hi, babe," Gerard said. "I didn't mean to awaken you. We were starved from being at the hospital all this time."

"Faith, what a day, girl. Gerard suggested I stay with you guys. I'm too much of a wreck over Elijah to stay in my motel alone," Iris said as though she and Faith were relatives.

Leaning in the doorway, Faith was speechless. She stood taking in the sight of Gerard and his ex-wife taking over her kitchen, and wondered if she was caught up in a bad dream. How dare Gerard invite this woman into their house without getting her permission?

Finally she found her voice. "How—how is Elijah?"

"He's afraid and was in pain. But after they ran tests on him and got him settled in his room, they gave him medication that knocked him out. We stayed until we were satisfied that he was comfortable for the night." Gerard finished making the hearty sandwich, sliced it in half and placed it on a plate for Iris. "Would you like the other half?" he asked his wife. "I can fix myself another."

"No, you eat it. I'm going to turn in for the night." She eyed the suitcases near the kitchen door, where Iris and Gerard had entered from the garage. The sight unnerved her. Then she marched off to her bedroom and shut the door. There she hopped on the bed, propped herself up and folded her arms. She couldn't believe what Gerard had done.

Soon Gerard appeared. He smiled weakly and proceeded to undress for bed.

"I can't believe you bought her here," she said, scowling at Gerard.

"I had no choice. She was pretty upset. It was the right thing to do for Elijah's sake," he said softly. "She won't be here long."

"And just how long are we talking about?"

Shirtless, Gerard sat down on the bed beside her. "She wants to stay until Elijah gets out the hospital. The doctor said if everything goes well, he should be home in a couple of days."

"You know I don't care for her. How am I supposed to feel at ease in my own home with her here?"

Looking defeated, Gerard said, "Can't you stop thinking about yourself for a minute? My son—Iris's son—was injured in a terrible accident. We're lucky that he wasn't hurt any worst than he was."

"Don't try and make me look like I'm the selfish one in this," Faith fumed. "Iris is the one who always shows up out the blue and wants everyone to stop the world for her and her life."

Gerard stared at her impatiently. "Iris feels awful that Elijah had to get hurt while he was with her," he said. "She confessed to me that things haven't been too good for her in her career and with her relationship with that guy named Legend."

225

"I thought she was setting world on fire," she said curtly. "I mean, she was doing something, because she sure didn't take time to call her own son or to get in touch with you to find out how her child was making out."

"He's mine, too. She knows I'm going to do what's right by him." Gerard sat upright and moved off the bed. His face revealed his grumpiness.

Faith turned away from him. He just didn't get how she felt about his forcing Iris on her by bringing her into their home. He was treating her as though she had no feelings or say in this matter because she wasn't a blood relation of Elijah.

"I bet you're trying to figure out a way to ask me if she's showed up to take him back with her, aren't you?" He unsnapped his jeans, stepped out of them and flung them into the corner.

"You don't know what I'm thinking and, believe me, nor do you want to know," she snapped. She flung the covers off of her and got out of bed. She strutted to the dresser, picked up a bottle of lotion and began to lubricate her hands in a wringing and angry manner.

Standing in his boxers, Gerard rubbed his eyes. "I'm beat. Iris is using Elijah's room," he informed her. "I'm going to try to get some sleep." He strode to the bed and climbed between the sheets. "We promised Elijah we'd be there as soon as we could in the morning. Iris and I are going to keep him company as much as we can until the doctor releases him to come home."

"One big happy family," Faith said coldly. "I have no place in your equation. You and she certainly have more common with one another than you and I do."

"Let it go, Faith. I can't do this now," Gerard grumbled, turning away from her.

She marched to the side of the bed and snatched the covers off of him.

"No, I want to do this now. If you ask me, our lives wouldn't be in this disorder except for Iris. What is the deal with her? Is she out to make sure that you and any other woman you have will have no happiness like you two did? Why won't she let you live your life in peace? Not only is she creating issues for you, but she is also toying with Elijah's feelings. You're going to have to put a stop to her thoughtlessness. I can't have her running in and out of our lives and leaving us to pick up the pieces." Her voice had risen in anger.

Gerard sat up on the side of the bed and lowered his head into his hands.

"I don't want to discuss Iris. She's here, and I intend to make her feel welcomed. After all, she and I are going to have to get along for our son's sake. I had the scare of my life when you called to tell me to get to the hospital, that Elijah had been in an accident. I only want to concentrate on getting him healthy and back home with me. I know you're threatened by Iris, but I can't deal with that at this point." He turned out the lamp on his side of the bed, lay down and tugged the covers over himself.

"You can't be serious. Someone like her doesn't pose a threat to me. If you want our marriage to last, I want you to get her straight. I want you to show more respect for me as your wife and for our marriage, which seems to have become secondary to you."

Faith didn't want to stay in the same room or bed with Gerard. She considered going into the guest room, but she didn't want to give Iris the satisfaction of thinking she had created a problem between them.

The next morning, Faith awoke before Gerard, showered, dressed and left for the mall to begin her workday at Fabulous. She didn't want to begin her day staring at Iris or watching Gerard eating breakfast with her, sitting by like an intruder in her own home. She sat in her office sipping coffee, sulking and feeling lonely.

Her cell phone rang, and she picked it up, noticing that it was Paula calling.

"Where are you? I called the house asking for you, and Gerard told me he had no idea where you had gone."

"He knows if I'm not home and not with you guys that I'm probably at Fabulous this early in the morning," Faith said.

"What's going on? I would expect you'd be

here at the hospital to visit Elijah. I came to work my shift a bit early so I could visit with him. He's asked for you," Paula informed her.

"Uh—tell him I'll be by to see him sometime today," Faith said. Hearing that Elijah had asked for her made her feel guilty for not insisting to see him. She had been so consumed over the presence of Iris and the way she had clung to Gerard, as though Faith hadn't mattered, that she had decided to step out of the situation all together.

"I will do that. There's something going on with you and Gerard," Paula said. "I can hear the sadness in your voice."

"We had words concerning Iris. He bought her home to live with us while Elijah's in the hospital. Iris claims she's distressed and doesn't want to be alone," she said dryly.

"Oh my goodness. No wonder you're out so early."

"How much more understanding am I to be, Paula? All the problems we've had since we've gotten married have been concerning her."

"I sympathize with you. But bear with it. This is certainly not the time to allow your feelings for that woman to interfere with your family— Gerard and Elijah," Paula chided. "Your focus should be on Elijah. The last thing he needs to feel is that he is causing trouble or may not be wanted."

Faith swallowed a lump of emotion. She couldn't respond to Paula to defend herself or to make her understand how tired she was of having to be the one to make things work. She wanted to be Gerard's wife and have his children. That was all she'd had in mind when she married him. She hadn't counted on all the complications that ruined the romantic times that should have been theirs as they got to know each other more intimately during their first year of marriage.

"I was talking to Elijah this morning while he was having breakfast, and he was telling me about the accident. He mentioned that his mom was on her cell phone, fussing with her boyfriend, Legend. That was the last thing he remembered before the crash."

"Say what?" Faith said, surprised by the information.

"From the sound of your voice, I can tell this is the first you've heard of this. Iris didn't admit to Gerard that she was using her cell phone."

"She isn't going to take responsibility for what happened. When I saw her in the emergency room, her story was that the weather was rainy, and a crazy driver had crashed into her car after she and Elijah were leaving the movies."

"Maybe she's afraid to let Gerard know. From what I've heard from you, and from the way Elijah has described his mother, leaving him here and there when they lived out of town, Iris makes me believe she is an irresponsible parent," Paula said.

"I don't know Iris very well, but I can tell when

someone doesn't have it together. I get the feeling she's hungry for all the wrong things in her life."

"She needs to decide whether she's going to be a good mother to Elijah. Gerard told me he would be by the hospital this morning. You should come too. Let Elijah know you care about him," she urged. "You and Gerard are at odds, but Elijah shouldn't suffer for that."

"I'll come later," she relented. "I want to handle a few things here and help Tasha open the store, and then I'll slip out to check on him."

"I'm going by Elijah's room to tell him. I'm sure he'll be glad to hear that. I'll talk with you, later."

Hanging up her phone, Faith took a deep breath. She wondered if she should mention to Gerard what Paula had told her concerning Iris being on her phone with her man and arguing during the horrible weather. She decided not to say anything. In due time, Iris was bound to reveal her shortcomings.

It was two o'clock that afternoon when Faith made her appearance in Elijah's room. He and his father were watching television. Elijah's eyes widened with surprise, and he grinned at her. Returning his smile, Faith had an unexpected surge of elation. Just like his father, Elijah had managed to charm his way into her heart these past few weeks. She went over to him, hugged him and kissed him on his forehead with real emotion for the first time since she'd known him.

"How are you feeling, little man?" Faith asked, caressing his face. She checked out the bandage near his eye and noticed that his arm was in a sling. "You've been through a lot. But you're going to be fine."

"I want to go home," Elijah said. "The food is yucky."

"You keep doing what the doctor and the nurses say, and you'll be out of here before you know it," Faith said.

Gerard sat forward in his seat, and his eyes sparkled at his wife's gestures.

"Hey," she said to Gerard. "How are things going?" She reached inside the tote bag she carried, removed a bag from the toy store and handed it to Elijah.

While Elijah dug into the bag and pulled out two of the action figures he had mentioned he wanted to complete his collection, Gerard got out of his seat and went to his wife. He kissed her on the face and gave her a tender look of appreciation.

"Step in the hallway with me for a minute," he said to her. "We'll be right in the hallway," Gerard told Elijah as they left him opening the packaged men.

"I haven't seen or heard anything from Iris today. I left her in bed. When I went to her room, she said she had some phone calls to make. I've called the house, but she isn't answering the phone," Gerard explained. "Elijah has been asking for her."

Instead of reproaching the woman's character, Faith shook her head.

"I've been trying to be patient and understanding of Iris. But I'm beginning to wonder about her now. I'm so glad she sought me out to help with Elijah. I hate to think what kind of care he had from her." He leaned his long form against the tile wall, looking dubious.

"I don't like the idea of her being left alone in our house. Maybe you should go check on her and drag her here where she should be."

"I'll give her another call in a minute. If she doesn't answer, I'll go see what's keeping her. She said she was going to get herself another rent-a-car to get around in."

Facing the room, Faith caught a glimpse of Elijah leaning forward in his bed as though he was trying to see if they were still there.

"We'd better get back with Elijah," she suggested. "We can keep him company until she decides to show up."

"Maybe this is her," Gerard announced, reaching for his cell phone and glancing at the caller ID. "Nope, not Iris. It's the bank calling me. It'd better be an emergency." He strode down the hall to return the call.

Faith took a seat by the bed and began a conversation with Elijah concerning the adventure he was creating with the action figures she'd bought him.

Gerard was gone for a couple of minutes. Returning, he turned to Faith. "Can you spare me an hour or two and stay with Elijah? I have to get to the bank. They need to open my computer files for a report that must be done today. I'm the only one with the password."

Reaching for Elijah's leg, Faith patted it. "Go on. I'll be here until you return. Tasha is quite capable of holding down things at Fabulous. Business will be a bit slow today anyway," she explained.

A look of relief flooded Gerard's face, and he winked at his wife. "You're a gem." Then he placed his hand on top of Elijah's head and looked him deep into the eyes. "I'll be back, kiddo. I'll sneak a milkshake in for you. How about that?"

Nodding his head, Elijah giggled.

"I'll check on you-know-who too," Gerard told Faith, and then he left the two alone.

She and Elijah watched cartoons until he fell asleep from the fresh pain patch the nurse administered to him for the ache he complained of in his cast-covered arm.

Faith even drifted off herself. Then she was startled awake by the loud entrance of Iris, who was carrying an oversized stuff animal and followed by her big, imposing boyfriend, Legend.

"There's my baby boy," Iris exclaimed, giving Faith a forced smile. "You look so much better than you did yesterday." She sat on the side of

Elijah's bed, took him in her arms to hug him and placed lipstick-smeared kisses on both of his cheeks.

The kid was groggy, but seemed happy to see his mother and the big bear she had propped up beside him.

"I thought you were coming earlier, Mom," Elijah said.

"Mommy had some business to take care of, baby. Then your uncle Legend flew in to be with me. He knew how upset I was over everything that had happened between us." She held out her hand to her man, pulled him to her side and rested her face against his broad chest. "Legend, doesn't he look great? Uncle Legend flew to town the minute he knew you and I were in trouble, baby."

Standing up and refusing to be disregarded anymore, Faith said, "Elijah has been asking for you. He thought you weren't coming. It's good to see you, Legend. I'm glad you're here for—Iris."

Nodding politely, the man smiled at Faith.

Iris eyed Faith, then turned her attention to Elijah. "Oh boy, you know I was going to get here. I was sure to lock the doors at the house. I won't need your hospitality now that my man is here. He's gotten us a hotel room."

Faith forced a smile. She was relieved that Iris would at least be out of her house.

"Have you felt any effects from the accidents yet?"

"Girl, I had some stiffness, but it's nothing I can't live with. I've got my baby with me, and he gives great massages. I had one before I came." She and Legend exchanged knowing looks that revealed more than therapy had occurred between them.

How could this woman, knowing her child was laid up in the hospital, take time for herself to be intimate with her man? What in the world was going on? Faith wondered. Hadn't Elijah told Paula that his mother had been arguing with Legend? But today he had showed up with her, acting as though they were teenage lovers.

"Where's Gerard?" Iris asked Faith.

"He's been here most of the day. He had to go to his office to deal with some details. He should be back soon," Faith said.

"Good. I need to talk to him. I hope he gets here soon. Legend and I had some things we need to do," Iris said.

Faith smiled politely and turned away from her and Legend, who were fawning over Elijah. She had a feeling that Iris was setting her son up to leave him again. She was consumed with annoyance over Iris's cavalier manner. How in the world could she desert her only child? If Faith had a child, no one could have separated her from her baby, especially if he was in the shape that Elijah was in.

After visiting Elijah and letting herself get to know him over the holidays, Faith had set aside the ridiculous bitterness she'd had because he had come into their lives unexpectedly. The child had been caught in the middle of an unfortunate situation created by his thoughtless mother. He had done nothing to Faith. In fact, he had stayed out of her way, probably out of fear of how she'd react to him.

Taking a small parental role in the eight-year-old boy's life and seeing him injured and afraid, yet requesting to see her in his condition, had touched Faith's heart.

Elijah, like any other child, was worthy of having a stable home filled with love, laughter and happiness. Obviously Iris didn't want to create that for her son. But Faith was willing to do so. Her late mother would expect nothing less of her. Her mother had been kind, loving and sensitive. And she wanted to make her mother proud by being that kind of woman too.

"Iris, I'd like to have a talk with you. There is a snack room down the hall where we can get a cup of coffee and chat," Faith said.

"Sure," Iris said with a smirk, looking at her man. "Legend, you don't mind keeping my baby company, do you?" She straightened the covers on her son's bed. Then she picked up her oversized designer purse and said, "Let's go, hon." She walked out of the room in a manner that showed Faith she wasn't intimidated by her.

And Faith surely wasn't afraid of her. Her husband hadn't confronted this woman, but she was more than ready to put an end to this situation.

CHAPTER SEVENTEEN

Reaching the snack room of the hospital, Faith was pleased to see that no one else was there. The two of them quietly served themselves coffee.

Faith took a seat at a table while Iris took her time sweetening her coffee with plenty of sugar and cream before she joined her.

Staring into the woman's tough eyes, Faith knew that if she wasn't careful, the conversation she planned could turn into an altercation. Although Iris was sexy and fairly pretty with the help of makeup and hair extensions, Faith knew that this was only a front for a lifestyle she hadn't been accustomed to, but truly hungered for.

"So, what do you have to say, Miss Faith?" Iris asked, staring at her deep red nails. "I had a feeling you were going to holla at me. I could tell by the expression on your face last night when I arrived at your crib that you didn't want me there."

"You're right. I didn't like the idea of you there.

239

I thought you were taking advantage of Gerard's kindness. I can't believe you were as distraught as you claimed to be. I believe you only wanted to see how much control you had over my husband." Faith sipped her coffee and studied the woman's reaction to her words.

"If you think I want Gerard back, you're on the wrong track. What I had for him faded years ago. My only concern is that I wanted a father for Elijah. I've seen too many boys get in trouble as they grow older, because they didn't know their dads."

"That's true. But why now? What took you eight long years to decide to bring Gerard into Elijah's life?" Faith stared at Iris.

Iris couldn't hold her stare. She gazed down into her cup and then slowly leveled her eyes, which had lost their bold luster, with Faith's.

"I love Elijah, but I've given him all that I can. I want something for myself other than being a mother working a wage-hour job. While I still have my looks, I want to be somebody special," she said fervently.

"And your son keeps you from becoming that," Faith said in a judgmental tone.

"Don't do that. I can tell from your tone that you think you know who I am, but you don't know me. You don't know where I come from or what I've seen or been through."

"That's exactly why I wanted to talk to you, so I can understand you. From what I do think I know of you, I don't respect you. But as a woman, I want to like you. You and I are sisters."

Iris laughed softly. "You're one of those fancy ladies who think I'm out to ruin that paradise you have with Gerard."

"You've come close to it. Gerard and I haven't even been married for a year and you've thrown enough curves in it to almost make me pack up and leave. I didn't marry Gerard to help raise another woman's child."

"If you don't like the situation, you ought to leave." Iris shrugged. "Life isn't always going be the way you plan. I'm sure Gerard and Elijah will be just fine without you and your negative attitude toward them."

"You'd love that, wouldn't you? Then you could just waltz in and out of Gerard's and Elijah's lives anytime you choose. Anytime things fall apart for you, you could come running back to Gerard for sympathy and a shoulder to lean on, because you are the mother of his son."

Iris gave Faith a smoldering look.

"I don't want Gerard. I don't want to live the uptight life you live with him. I've got a man. Legend is a rapper and a record promoter too now. He loves me. He's going to marry me and give me everything I've always wanted."

"Things. That's all you want, is things. What about the things money can't buy? I might live an uptight life, but I have love in my life. I have the love of my family, my husband, and if you keep running away from your son, I'm sure he's going to find a place in his heart for me, too. There was a time when I didn't want that. But Elijah is a good boy with a good heart, and I'd be proud to call him son and to give him sisters or brothers."

Iris gave Faith a seething look. "My baby will love me, and I'll always love him no matter where I am."

"That may be true, Iris. But you're taking a risk. You stay away too long, he'll come to resent you for not being around when he needs you the most."

Iris rubbed the side of her face thoughtfully. Her bottom lip quivered. She bolted out of her seat and away from the table, and went over to the snack machine and leaned against it, her head lowered and her back to Faith.

Gerard entered the snack room and caught a glimpse of Iris hovering in the corner. He stared at Faith, who sat with her arms folded, looking somber.

"What's going on here?"

Iris turned to show Gerard her tear-stained face. He went to her and slid an arm around her waist. "Faith, what's been going on? What did you say?"

"She and I were only having a woman-to-woman talk. Obviously she didn't like the truth I spoke," Faith said coolly.

"What did you say?" Gerard asked his wife, looking concerned.

"You ask her. It's apparent that my words don't matter to you anymore." She got up and walked out of the room. She returned to Elijah's hospital room, where her coat and purse were. She gave Elijah a kiss on the cheek and told him she'd see him later. She left the room and made her way to the nearest exit.

Gerard came up beside her. "Let's talk. Don't leave," he urged, taking her hand.

"I've said all I wanted to for today. I won't have you chastising me over what I should and shouldn't say to Iris. You stay with your family." Her voice broke slightly. She removed her hand out of his grip and walked away from him. She heard him curse out of frustration.

Leaving the hospital to return to Fabulous, Faith was caught in the evening rush-hour traffic. Sitting in traffic, she was hit with all kinds of thoughts. She didn't want to dislike Iris, but she didn't favor the way she was attempting to get away from him. She had tried not to like Elijah, but she realized she had been wrong. Elijah had bought a joy into her and Gerard's lives. He had filled them with an enchanting energy that couldn't be disregarded.

Elijah was a child who loved to watch television or listen and sing off-key along to music on the radio or his CD player. Faith had grown comfortable with the sight of the eight-year-old sprawled on the floor of their den, working on his homework or playing with his video games. In her stolen glances, she admired the way Gerard and Elijah tussled with each other. Yes, Gerard was born to be a father and a husband, though she hadn't shown him how much she cherished those wonderful qualities. Just as she and her husband would get close, Iris would do something that would divide them.

She regarded Iris as selfish. Who was Faith to judge her, though? Faith silently questioned herself. Her behavior with the child hadn't been admirable. According to Gerard, Iris's lack of appreciation and consideration had ended their marriage Gerard had been a good husband and a wonderful lover, and had proven he could be a devoted father with Elijah. She was truly blessed to have him in her life; she had to begin showing him she felt this way.

Entering Fabulous, Faith was amazed by the amount of business that was taking place. Tasha had a line of customers, and she had only two of their part-time helpers assisting her.

Faith went behind the counter to an available cash register to clear up the customers who needed help. She was grateful to be busy. Work would be a salve to her anxieties.

At nine o'clock, when the store closed, Faith wore a broad, weary grin. No one could tell how conflicted she was on the inside. After thirty minutes, Faith told the part-time workers they could leave for the night. Left alone with Tasha, she felt more relaxed and at ease. She leaned on the counter and looked at the stuff that still had to be reshopped.

"I wish you had called me, Tasha. I could have left the hospital. Elijah is coming along nicely," Faith said.

"I was all right," she said. "Family comes first, lady." She kicked off her shoes and sat on a stool near Faith. "We did good business this evening, boss lady. It seems like everyone chose this evening to come redeem their gift certificates and use holiday money." She laughed.

"I'm grateful for whatever bought them in. I'm pleased that Fabulous is growing popular." Faith yawned and stretched with the fatigue of her long day.

Thinking of how she had left the hospital on a bad note with Gerard, the euphoria of her day began to fade. She didn't know what to expect when she went home. Was it going to be a night of silent tension or yet another confrontation over his ex?

"Let's take these things left over from this evening into the back and put them away tomorrow. Then you and I can go home and get the rest we deserve like the part-time workers."

"Those college girls you hired are something else, aren't they?" Tasha began to stack her arms with clothes to place in the storeroom. "All they talk about are men. They have them on the brain." She chuckled. "I certainly hope they don't lose focus on their studies because of a man. I told them to be like you, Faith. You're a perfect role model for them. Yes, you are."

"That's kind of you to say that. But I'm not all of that. I have my faults, my problems," she said in a worn-out tone.

"Heck, you're my idol. You're a young woman who has her own business. You're pretty inside and out, and smart as a whip. Landed yourself a good man whom I can tell worships you."

Over an armful of tops and jeans, Faith smiled nervously at Tasha. "Oh yeah, I am a lucky woman," she said, though she felt far from that at the moment, with her heart in turmoil.

Faith entered her darkened house to the incessant ringing of her telephone. She dropped her things at the door and dashed for it, praying it would be Gerard, with whom she was ready to compromise to make things better.

"Hello?" Faith answered excitedly.

"This is Iris. Can I speak to Gerard?" she asked in a cool tone, with a hint of arrogance.

"I just arrived from work. Maybe he's still at the hospital," she said, wondering why Iris wasn't there herself.

"No, he and I left early tonight. The nurse gave Elijah some medication that made him sleepy and suggested we let him rest. I have no idea where he is. I tried to call his cell phone, but all I get is his voice mail. I hope he is all right."

Hearing this, Faith grew concerned. With his son in the hospital, why wouldn't Gerard answer his phone?

"Well, when you hear from him, have him call me. He has my cell number," Iris said. Then she hung up abruptly.

Iris's rudeness didn't bother Faith. She wanted her off the line so she could check around for her husband. The first person she called was Alex.

"Alex, is my husband there?" she asked without even greeting him.

"He is," he said.

"May I speak to him?"

"Uh—that's not possible. The man got wasted and passed out. He's asleep in his old room."

"He's been drinking?" she asked, as though she hadn't understood what she heard.

"Exactly. Both of us have. He did more than me. It was like he was trying to medicate himself. I sure you know what he's been going through. Elijah is going to be released from the hospital tomorrow," he informed her. "Would you like me to go with him?"

"No, I'll go with him. Take care of him for the night, Alex. I'll come get him around ten or eleven in the morning."

"I'll tell him. He should have his head together by then. I'll leave a house key for you under my mat at the front door for you to let yourself in," Alex said. "I'm expected at work first thing in the morning."

"I understand. Thanks for everything," she said. "Good night."

Hanging up the phone and thinking of Gerard's passed-out condition, she felt as though she wanted to cry. Gerard wasn't the kind of man to get drunk. His limit was usually a two-drink maximum of liquor or maybe a couple of beers. She believed that today had really pushed him over the edge. He had managed to hold it together all these months with all the shenanigans with her and Iris. But going through the fright of Elijah being in the auto accident, and then the constant discord with Faith and Iris, had finally driven him to drink to escape the problems dumped on his lap.

Worried and restless, Faith made her way into the master bedroom and undressed, then drew a warm bath with lavender salts. Submerging herself in the tub, she hoped to find comfort. Closing her eyes to relax, Faith realized how naïve she'd been when she got married. How foolish she was to think she was going to have a fairy-tale life with Gerard. Fairy tales weren't real. Her new marriage, with all of its ups and downs, was most definitely reality. In months, she felt she had matured and become a stronger woman for all she'd been through. It was time she faced the fact that she wasn't unique and had no special formula for a perfect life. She had been wrong to expect Gerard to make the challenges they had to face go away, because of her idealistic expectations of what married life comprised. She regretted how insensitive she had been to her man, and she began to sob, thinking how lonely and helpless he must have felt dealing with the things that had come his way.

CHAPTER EIGHTEEN

The next morning, Faith arrived at Alex's place and let herself with the hidden key. She expected that Gerard would still be in bed, but he came out of the kitchen in pajama bottoms and a T-shirt, looking as though he felt miserable. He carried a mug of coffee.

"Morning," he greeted her in a husky tone.

"Good morning." She went to him and slid an arm around his waist. "I sure could use some of that coffee."

"Help yourself," he said. "There's plenty." He followed her as she made her way into Alex's kitchen.

"Is Elijah still being released today?" she asked, pouring her drink.

"I spoke with the hospital pediatrician and he told me I could get him before noon." He sipped on his drink, eyeing his wife, who wore jeans and a blouse. "You're not dressed for work."

"I'm not going in today. I'm going with you to the hospital to bring Elijah home and to help you get him settled." She drank her coffee, watching her husband stare at her.

"I appreciate that," he said, grinning slowly. He turned thoughtful, and then he said, "I'm glad you came. I have something I have to tell you."

"What's happened now?"

He set aside his mug and sat in the nearest chair. "After you left yesterday, Iris told me she and Legend had plans to leave for Saint-Tropez. She said Elijah was doing fine and she wasn't worried about him, because he had you and me to take care of him."

"Oh, I can't believe her."

"That not even the cream on top. She and Legend are getting married there. He has produced an album and will be releasing his own soon. She's in heaven with his success. It seems she wants to hook him before he becomes too big of a star. Also, while she's in Saint-Tropez, she has been signed to model bikinis for some men's magazine. So her life is definitely too busy to mother a child who is recuperating from injuries from an auto accident."

"And one that I suspect was caused by her carelessness. Paula spoke to Elijah the other day, and he told her his mother was arguing with Legend on her cell phone when the car crashed into them in the rainy weather."

"What?" Gerard exclaimed. "This is the first I

heard of this. Why didn't he tell me this?" He jumped out of his seat and hit his hand with his fist. "She never took responsibility for that."

"Calm down, Gerard," Faith urged, seeing the veins stand out on his neck.

"I am so glad she has decided to give me sole custody of Elijah. When you left the other day, she asked me to get a lawyer to draw up the papers for her to sign. Can you believe her? Can you imagine how Elijah is going to feel when he is able to understand all of this?"

"It's a shame. But we can't linger on that. We'll deal with that when the time is more appropriate. Has she left yet?"

"She is going to spend time with Elijah this morning, and then she and her man will be on their way to do their thing. That's why I'm not in a rush to get there. I can't bear to look at her and see the way she's treating my boy."

Faith listened quietly.

Gerard returned to the chair and sat, looking somber. "I'm not ever going to desert him. I know that feeling. I've been there, and it's a painful place. I remember when my mother left me for my grandmother to rear. She made me believe she was going away to make a better life for us. She told me that when she returned, we were going to have a wonderful life. But that never happened. She'd given me up for men and life on the streets," he said, as though the hurtful memory was still fresh.

Faith had known Gerard's mother had died, but whenever she tried to get him to tell her the full story, he'd shut down on her. It wasn't until that moment that she heard the full story of his pain. It saddened her to know that he had been in such a grim situation. Like an epiphany, it became apparent why Gerard had been so adamant about assuming his role in Elijah's life when he had learned he was the boy's father.

Faith went to him, looped her arms around his neck and tenderly kissed the top of his head.

He reached up and stroked her arm. "Don't pity me, baby. I survived, didn't I?" He was silent. Then he said, "I used to be bitter, but it served no purpose. My grandmother encouraged me to put that behind me, and I did. When I grew older, my grandmother explained that my mother had gotten mixed up with the wrong guy in her life who led her astray and into an early death." He cleared his throat. "What's important to me is that I've made my grandmother proud of the man I've become in spite of everything. I owe her so much for all her love and guidance." There was a brief pause. Then he said, "I swore to myself that if I ever was blessed with children, I would be there for them. They wouldn't have to grow up doubting whether I wanted or loved them." His voice was soft, yet full of determination.

The intimacy of their conversation filled Faith with hope. She took a seat on his lap, rested her face on his chest and held him.

"I'm sorry I was uncooperative in the beginning with Elijah. Forgive me for being selfish," she said.

He breathed deeply and held on to her as though he was absorbing hope and strength to face his challenges.

"I bought you a change of clothes," Faith said, moving off his lap. She pulled him to his feet with a smile that he matched. "Get a shower and get dressed so we can pick up Elijah. Come on, he's going to be expecting us."

Once they had gotten Elijah home and he had rested a bit, her father and Paula came by for a visit and to offer their help.

While Elijah rested on the couch that served as a temporary bed for the evening, Gerard and Rufus kept him company while watching a game on television.

Faith and Paula sat in the kitchen, drinking coffee and finishing off slices of chocolate cake Paula had made for Elijah's homecoming.

During a break in their conversation about Monica and her new boyfriend, whom Paula and Rufus liked so much better, Paula reached out and touched Faith's arm. "I'm proud of the way you're pulling your family together. I know all of this isn't fair, and how much you had to compromise to reach this place in your life. But this is life. When you marry someone, their problems become yours too. Sweet Elijah is here and in our lives. You have to give Gerard credit for doing a bang-up job of falling right into place of being an excellent father."

Faith's mouth curved into a smile. "He is that. I can't deny that. I've been wrong. I haven't been a good wife. At times I've withheld affection and sex because I was so completely undone. If Gerard chooses, he has grounds to file for a divorce after this thing we've gone through."

Giving Faith an encouraging look, Paula said, "Any other man might do that, but Gerard is a special breed of man. He shows he believes in family, and most importantly, he proved how much he loved you with his patience and his refusal to let you out of his life. You should be glad you have him."

"I am. I know this more than ever," Faith responded. Her eyes gleamed with the love she had for her husband.

"This is over. You can't dwell on it or fret him about it. Also, forgive yourself for your behavior. You're only human."

"You're right. What with Iris's plans of getting married to Legend and flying to France for a honeymoon and a modeling assignment, Gerard and I have nothing to do but move forward. Gerard will have full custody of Elijah. His mother has made it clear she doesn't want the responsibility of the growing boy anymore."

"I can't believe that woman. Poor Elijah. I'm glad you're ready to mother him," Paula said.

"You're going to be good for him, and he's going to grow to love you for it. That's priceless, you know. I'm sure your mother would be proud of the woman you've grown into."

Hearing Paula kindly mention her mother touched Faith. Tears welled in her eyes, and she leaned toward Paula, threw her arms around her and hugged her in a manner she had never done. With dewy eyes, Paula returned her stepdaughter's affection.

Breaking their embrace and wiping her tears, Faith said, "I'm sorry for the way I've treated you through the years. You've been a godsend to me. Just think, it took trouble in my marriage for me to appreciate you. It means a lot to me to have a woman like you to confide in and encourage me. I—I love you."

Paula smiled. "I'm glad you feel that way. I'm glad that you and I have become close. It's what I've prayed for. I know your mother has a dear place in your heart, but I'm honored to share your love too."

Faith's words freed her from all the secret insecurities she'd clung to all these years. Cheerfulness brightened her eyes, and she was infused by a feeling of warmth that limbered her body. Paula had never tried to keep her away from her father. In the past few weeks of introspection, Faith recognized she had been the one who had allowed her imagination to create the battle for her father's affection that never really was. And how ridiculous had she been to expect Gerard to choose her over his son? A moment's shame pulsed through her.

Suddenly her father appeared. He placed a hand on Faith's shoulder and squeezed it affectionately.

"Elijah is going to be just fine. He was a bit sleepy, so Gerard tucked him into bed," Rufus said.

"He's had quite a day," Faith said, moving out of her seat and clearing the table.

"I suppose you and I should leave. I'm sure Faith and Gerard could use some rest too," Paula said, standing and hugging her husband.

"Is there anything you'd like for us to do?" Rufus asked.

"No, we'll be okay," Faith said, smiling.

"If you want anything, don't be afraid to give us a call," Paula said. "Let's get our coats and let these folks have some privacy." She winked at Faith and herded her husband toward the front door where their things were.

"I'm sorry I didn't get a chance to tell Paula and Rufus good night. It was great of them to come over. Elijah liked them stopping by. They made him feel special," Gerard said.

Faith was in the family room, picking up here and there. "Is he resting comfortably with that arm?"

"He's fine," he assured her.

"Let's go hang out in the kitchen, so we can

have some refreshments and talk," he suggested with that charming smile of his.

"Okay. Today you can have your choice of whatever it is you want."

Dressed in the form-fitting jeans she knew he loved on her, Faith led the way, placing an extra bit of sway in her hips. "I took time and stocked up on groceries earlier so we could have the kind of goodies that you and Elijah have been missing lately."

Gerard went to the fridge and opened it. "Wow! We haven't had this much food since we first stocked up when we returned from our honeymoon." He reached for a cold beer and closed the door, watching Faith as she watered the plants in the kitchen window. His eyes were glued to her goddesslike body. He knew how wonderful her smooth and taut flesh felt next to his, and his male essence strained against the zipper of his jeans. He yearned to get lost in her and to share his loving spirit with her the way he used to when she had thought nothing of surrendering her all to him. He took a gulp of his beer to cool his erotic thoughts. He didn't want to rush her into bed yet. But he was hoping their evening would end with them nude and in one another's arms.

Encouraged that his eyes were on her, Faith washed her hands and poured herself another cup of coffee. She carried her mug to the table, sat and signaled for him to join her. "What would you like to talk about first?"

Striding over to the table, Gerard took one of the chairs, turned it backward and straddled it. Gulping his beer, he stared at her intently. "I don't know where to begin. You and I have been through quite a journey to return back to where we began."

She sighed. "It has been something else. But I'm pleased that we can begin to put our life back together, and with Elijah. I regret everything I've said or done, learning you were a father to Iris's child. To be honest with you, I was threatened by Iris."

Gerard set his can of beer aside and folded his arms on the back of the chair. "You've never had anything to be concerned about. I had no feelings that way for Iris. You should have seen that from the beginning. On the other hand, I loved my son from the moment I laid eyes on him and had him grin at me. What I feel is totally different from what you and I have. I love you with my all my heart and soul. I can't say that enough."

Pressing her hands on the table, she met his gaze. "And I feel exactly the same way, babe." Her voice was soft, sexy and full of conviction.

He took her hand and urged her out her chair and onto his lap. "I'm pleased to know that. Remember, when all this drama reared its head, that I said I had more than enough love for you, Elijah and any other children we may bring into the world. That's a guarantee you can count on." He snuggled his head on her breasts and relished the soft cushionlike feel.

Faith touched his face as though it were an amazing piece of bronze sculpture, and kissed his lips. "I love you so," she whispered against his lips. "I'm so glad that we've overcome our problems. After what we've been through, I think we can deal with anything."

Relief flooded Gerard's face. He placed his hand behind her neck and gave her a lingering kiss that was full of heated fervor. He ended the kiss and held his face next to hers. "We have turned everything around. I knew you had a good heart and would come around. It was bruised and clouded by your emotions. I knew the real woman I married and fell in love with would emerge eventually."

"But it was also my pain that helped me to understand what real love and commitment is. I don't know about you, but I've come out of all of this stronger and more determined to hold on to what we have." She offered him a bright smile to show how sincere she was. "Have you decided how you're going to tell Elijah about the arrangements his mother has made with you concerning him?"

"No, I haven't. But I know you'll help make easier for me and him. You and I'll make sure he'll be fine, even though I'm sure he's going to be hurt."

She hugged him. "You can count on me. That's

my guarantee to you. I will also make sure Elijah understands I honestly care for him."

Gerard's eyes glistened with tears of joy and amazement. He caressed her face as though he were seeing her for the first time. "You have grown more beautiful with each passing day." He spoke as though he was in awe. His mouth eased into a mischievous grin. "I want that baby with you more than ever. I'd like to begin production as soon as possible."

Faith's face radiated with joy. "Hey, I'm as ready as you are."

Laughing with delight, the couple entwined their arms around each other, kissing and caressing to quench their denied desires. Their breathing intensified, and clothes were stripped away and tossed haphazardly around the kitchen.

Frustrated by the limitations of sitting in the chair, Gerard rose from his seat, cradling his wife in his strong arms, and hurried off to their bed.

Between the sheets, where they melded their hot, yearning flesh, Faith and Gerard renewed the passion and the glorious love they'd known and spoken of. In Gerard's arms, Faith felt her spirit and soul being revitalized. Reflected in his wife's eyes, Gerard saw the endearing love he had missed and craved. He truly felt he had returned home. Lying together with their hearts beating in harmony, the Wynns knew they would always have more than enough love to defeat anyone or anything that dared come between them or their family. They had learned together that they had a power more precious than gold.

When spring arrived that year, Gerard and Faith were more in love than ever. They were proud of their son, Elijah, who was well mannered and always full of silly jokes or antics to keep them in good humor. Now that winter had passed, the Wynns decided to venture out each weekend on family trips. Their first outing was in the park to enjoy the warmth of the sun and the fragrance of the flowers in bloom.

Sitting on a blanket spread on the ground, Faith watched Gerard and Elijah having the time of their lives tossing a Frisbee back and forth. Elijah was better at this than Gerard had anticipated. The boy took pleasure in being able to make tosses with the arm he had broken, but which had healed healthy and strong enough to challenge his father at his agility in catching. Smiling at the two men in her life, Faith rubbed her tummy. She was two months pregnant, and in tip-top condition according to her doctor. Faith felt glee on this spring day, experiencing the joy and love of her evergrowing family. The love to which she had opened her heart made Faith feel special—a woman who had grown stronger from all her yesterdays.

A MOMENT ON THE LIPS

PHYLLIS BOURNE WILLIAMS

Grant Price wants old classmate Melody Mason to work for his family's Boston investment company. Melody has retired from big business and is hiding. It is Grant's assignment to lure her back to the fast life. But when he arrives at her door, she doesn't look like the woman he remembers....

Melody has hidden herself away in rural Tennessee for a reason: she desperately needed a life change. So she has no intention of returning to a fast-paced lifestyle. Instead, she makes Grant an offer: stay, relax and find out what life is like without a hectic pace. Unfortunately, real life calls and Grant must return to Boston. Can Grant and Melody agree on what a good life truly means?

- -

Dorchester Publishing Co., Inc.
P.O. Box 6640   ___5659-3
Wayne, PA 19087-8640   **$6.99 US/$8.99 CAN**

Please add $2.50 for shipping and handling for the first book and $.75 for each additional book. NY and PA residents, add appropriate sales tax. No cash, stamps, or CODs. Canadian orders require $2.00 for shipping and handling and must be paid in U.S. dollars. Prices and availability subject to change. **Payment must accompany all orders.**

Name: _____

Address: _____

City: _____ State: _____ Zip: _____

E-mail: _____

I have enclosed $_____ in payment for the checked book(s).

CHECK OUT OUR WEBSITE! www.dorchesterpub.com
____ Please send me a free catalog.

JENNIE KLASSEL
IT HAPPENED IN SOUTH BEACH

If she's a beauteous, bodacious babe, gettin' down, gettin' it on, gettin' her man, she's definitely *not* good old Tilly Snapp. So what's the safe, sensible twenty-six-year-old Bostonian doing in Miami's ultra-hip, super-chic South Beach?

She's on the trail of the fabled Pillow Box of Win Win Poo—the most valuable collection of antique erotic "accessories" in the world. And she's after the fiend who murdered her eccentric Aunt Ginger. And while Tilly might not know the difference between a velvet tickle pickle and a kosher dill, with the assistance of the sexy yet unhelpful Special Agent Will Maitland, she's about to get a crash course in sex-ed.

Meet the new Tilly Snapp, Sex Detective.

South Beach ain't seen nothin' yet.

Dorchester Publishing Co., Inc.
P.O. Box 6640
Wayne, PA 19087-8640

_____52635-2
$5.99 US/$7.99 CAN

Please add $2.50 for shipping and handling for the first book and $.75 for each additional book. NY and PA residents, add appropriate sales tax. No cash, stamps, or CODs. Canadian orders require an extra $2.00 for shipping and handling and must be paid in U.S. dollars. Prices and availability subject to change. **Payment must accompany all orders.**

Name: _____

Address: _____

City: _____ State: _____ Zip: _____

E-mail:_____

I have enclosed $_____ in payment for the checked book(s).
CHECK OUT OUR WEBSITE! **www.dorchesterpub.com**
_____ Please send me a free catalog.

TAKE YOUR PICK!

SUBSCRIBE NOW AND SAVE 50% OFF THE NEWSSTAND PRICE!

Start my subscription to **Right On!** & **Black Beat** Now!

12 BIG ISSUES
(6 of each) For $29.95

☐ **SPECIAL COMBO OFFER $29.95!—** A Great Deal & Save 50%!!!

BEST DEAL

☐ 6/$19.94

☐ 6/$19.94

☐ I perfer only one magazine at this time.

Name _____ (Please print)

Address _____ Apt. #

City _____ State _____ Zip _____ J6MOS.

PAYMENT ENCLOSED ☐ **BILL ME** ☐ Charge my VISA ☐ MASTERCARD ☐ DISCOVER ☐ AMERICAN EXPRESS ☐
(Check Or Money Order)

Make checks payable to Dorchester Media. Add $10.00 for Canadian & Foreign postage. (US Funds Only)

ACCT.# _____

Signature _____

Expiration _____

For Credit Card Orders Call 1-800-666-8783

PLEASE NOTE: Credit card payments for your subscription will appear on your statement as *Dorchester Media*, *not* as the magazine name.

Mail this coupon with check or credit card information to this address:

RIGHT ON! & BLACK BEAT
P.O. Box 5624
HARLAN, IOWA 51593-3124

JENNIFER ASHLEY
CONFESSIONS
of a
LINGERIE ADDICT

The fixation began on New Year's Day: Silky, expensive slips from New York and Italy. Camisoles and thongs from Beverly Hills. Before, Brenda Scott would have blushed to be caught dead in them. Now, she's ditched the shy and mousy persona that got her dumped by her rich and perfect fiancé, and she is sexy. Underneath her sensible clothes, Brenda is the woman she wants to be.

After all, why can't she be wild and crazy? Nick, the sexy stranger she met on New Year's, already seems to think she is. Of course, he didn't know the old Brenda. How long before Nick strips it all away and finds the truth beneath? And would that be a bad thing?

Dorchester Publishing Co., Inc.
P.O. Box 6640
Wayne, PA 19087-8640

___52636-0
$6.99 US/$8.99 CAN

Please add $2.50 for shipping and handling for the first book and $.75 for each additional book. NY and PA residents, add appropriate sales tax. No cash, stamps, or CODs. Canadian orders require an extra $2.00 for shipping and handling and must be paid in U.S. dollars. Prices and availability subject to change. **Payment must accompany all orders.**

Name: _____

Address: _____

City: _____ State: _____ Zip: _____

E-mail: _____

I have enclosed $_____ in payment for the checked book(s).

CHECK OUT OUR WEBSITE! www.dorchesterpub.com
_____ *Please send me a free catalog.*

ATTENTION
BOOK LOVERS!

Can't get enough of your favorite **ROMANCE**?

Call **1-800-481-9191** to:

✳ order books,

✳ receive a **FREE** catalog,

✳ join our book clubs to **SAVE 30%**!

Open Mon.-Fri. 10 AM-9 PM EST

Visit **www.dorchesterpub.com**
for special offers and inside
information on the authors you love.

We accept Visa, MasterCard or Discover®.
LEISURE BOOKS ♥ LOVE SPELL